Tudor Chronicles

The King in Blood Red and Gold

TERRY DEARY

Dolphin Paperbacks

First published in Great Britain in 1997
as an Orion hardback
and a Dolphin paperback

This new edition published 2005 by Dolphin paperbacks
a division of the Orion Publishing Group Ltd
Orion House
5 Upper St Martin's Lane
London WC2H 9EA

Printed in Great Britain by Clays Ltd, St Ives plc

ISBN 1 84255 139 6

www.orionbooks.co.uk

The King in Blood Red and Gold

Terry Deary was born in Sunderland and now lives in County Durham, where the Marsdens of *Tudor Chronicles* lived. Once an actor, he has also been a teacher of English and drama and has led hundreds of workshops for children in schools. He is the author of the bestselling *Horrible Histories* and of many other successful books for children, both fiction and non-fiction.

Also available

The Prince of Rags and Riches

Coming soon

The Lady of Fire and Tears
The Knight of Stars and Storms

Contents

All chapter titles are quotations from *Macbeth*. This play was written by William Shakespeare for King James the Sixth of Scotland and the First of England, a few years after the events of this book.

The Marsden Family   vii

CHAPTER ONE   1
"I have lived long enough"

CHAPTER TWO   9
"I am in blood steeped in so far"

CHAPTER THREE   21
"I have supped full with horrors"

CHAPTER FOUR   28
"So foul and fair a day I have nor seen"

CHAPTER FIVE   39
"Peep through the blanket of the dark"

CHAPTER SIX   45
"Methought I heard a voice cry, 'Sleep no more!'"

CHAPTER SEVEN   54
"I have almost forgot the taste of fears"

CHAPTER EIGHT   66
"False face must hide what the false heart doth know"

CHAPTER NINE   77
"Atleast we'll die with harness on our backs"

CHAPTER TEN   85
"And fixed his head upon our battlements"

CHAPTER ELEVEN 95
"Blood will have blood"

CHAPTER TWELVE 109
"Something wicked this way comes"

CHAPTER THIRTEEN 117
"That tears shall drown the wind"

CHAPTER FOURTEEN 127
"WHen the battle's lost and won"

CHAPTER FIFTEEN 138
"Upon the next tree thou shalt hang alive"

CHAPTER SIXTEEN 146
"Enter sir, the castle"

CHAPTER SEVENTEEN 153
"The night is long that never finds the day"

CHAPTER EIGHTEEN 163
"Hang out our banners on the outward walls"

CHAPTER NINETEEN 168
"I'll fight till from my bones my flesh be hacked"

CHAPTER TWENTY 175
*"Light thickens, and the crow makes wing
towards the rooky wood"*

The Historical Characters 180

The Time Trail 182

The Marsden Family

WILLIAM MARSDEN *The narrator*
The youngest member of the family. Training to be a knight as his ancestors were before him, although the great days of knighthood are long gone. His father insists on it and Great-Uncle George hopes for it. But he'd rather be an actor like the travelling players he has seen in the city. He can dream.

Grandmother **LADY ELEANOR MARSDEN**
She was a lady-in-waiting to Queen Anne Boleyn. After seeing the fate of her mistress she came to hate all men, she married one, maybe out of revenge. Behind her sharp tongue there is a sharper brain. She is wiser than she looks.

Grandfather **SIR CLIFFORD MARSDEN**
He was a soldier in Henry VIII's army where (Grandmother says) the batterings softened his brain. Sir Clifford is the head of the family although he does not manage the estate these days he simply looks after the money it makes. He is well known for throwing his gold around like an armless man.

Great-Uncle SIR GEORGE SULGRAVE

A knight who lost his lands and now lives with his stepsister, Grandmother Marsden. He lives in the past and enjoys fifty-year-old stories as much as he enjoys fifty-year-old wine. He never lets the truth stand in the way of a good story.

SIR JAMES MARSDEN *William's father*

He runs the Marsden estate and is magistrate for the district. He believes that, without him, the forces of evil would take over the whole of the land. This makes him a harsh and humourless judge. As a result he is as popular as the plague.

LADY MARSDEN *William's mother*

She was a lady-in-waiting to Mary Queen of Scots. Then she married Sir James. No one quite knows why. She is beautiful, intelligent, caring and witty. Quite the opposite of her husband and everyone else in the house.

MARGARET "MEG" LUMLEY

Not a member of the family, but needs to be included for she seems to be involved in all the family tales. A poor peasant and serving girl, but bright, fearless and honest (she says). Also beautiful under her weather-stained skin and the most loyal friend any family could wish for (she says).

"I have lived long enough"

I remember that evening when the crow circled over the garden of Marsden Hall. My family had gathered there after supper, as we often did when the weather was fine. We walked, we sat in the sheltered warmth of the end of the day and we shared stories. But that evening we had all stopped and looked up at the sunset sky of copper and gold and watched the crow in the still silence.

"One," my grandmother said. Her face was so pale with white make-up that it reflected back the amber sun and turned a curious shade of orange. The creases in her thin lips were straight and black.

"It's nonsense," my grandfather said softly. "Old women and witches believe that sort of gossip." But he didn't take his eye off the black bird. He looked like a black bird himself. A shrunken figure in a bat-black cloak, despite the warmth of the evening.

The crow turned its head so it seemed to be staring down at us.

"Two," my grandmother said, as it finished its second large circle around the west tower of the ancient house.

Great-Uncle George, my grandmother's stepbrother, stroked his thick white beard and chuckled. "She knows the way of crows," he told my grandfather. "She's even beginning to look like one!"

"It's a well-known fact," said my grandmother, "if a crow flies three times round the house against the course of the sun then it means a death."

A slight breeze sprang up from somewhere and lifted the bird; it rocked and steadied itself with a ripple of the feathers of one wing. It turned sharply inwards and flew towards the garden where we were sitting on the heavy oak benches round the lawn.

"Three," my father said briskly. He seemed to be looking along his thin, pinched nose even though the crow was high above us. His sharp beard pointed upwards over his crisp white ruff. He looked around the family sourly. His eyes hovered like the crow's over the three oldest people – Grandmother, Grandfather and Great-Uncle George. "I wonder who it's going to be?" he said.

It was a stupid and thoughtless thing to say. It was the sort of thing we would have expected from my father. He was loathed by every tenant on the Marsden estate. When he wasn't squeezing rents and taxes from the workers, he was bullying the beggars and the thieves. As a landlord he was grasping and mean. As magistrate for the district he was generous ... generous with the whip, the stocks and the hanging rope.

My mother had been crouching beside her rose bushes, plucking off the old blossoms to let the last of the year's blooms show through. Her hands were filled with faded petals. "It could be Her Majesty Queen Elizabeth," she suggested quickly. "Lately the news from London has all been about her failing health."

The crow gave a harsh cry and landed on top of the West

Tower. "No," my grandmother said. "It's come for one of us. You can see it seeking out its victim now."

As I looked up I felt its bright eyes were looking straight at me. No one thought I'd be the one to die. After all, I was only a boy.

No one expected me to be the one to die. Not even me. But something about that shuffling, hunched shape on the tower top made me shiver. Perhaps I should have taken more notice of the old superstitions.

Most evenings at Marsden Hall we told stories. Someone would say, "I remember when ..." and we'd all settle down to listen. Somehow I felt that the story that evening would be a grim one. There was no breeze inside the high stone walls and the hedged garden of Marsden Hall; but a September evening in the north east of England could suddenly turn cold. I thought perhaps that was what made me shiver.

Now that the crow had finished its three circles my grandmother relaxed. She gave a thin-lipped grin. "If you've come for me, I'm ready, my old friend," she said to the crow.

"Yes!" Great-Uncle George roared. "Come and take her! Give us all a little peace!"

It was hard to tell how serious the old man and his step-sister were. My mother looked distressed by this joking about death. She cared enough about them to worry about losing them.

But it was my grandfather who surprised me. The old man was looking up at the sunset sky, and I saw something in the small, deep eyes that I'd never seen before. A sort of fear.

Grandfather and I had never been close. He never tired of telling the family that young people these days were a disgrace. "Idle, dishonest and weak," he would snap. "And no respect for the old. They should remember that if it wasn't for us they wouldn't be here! We fought and died so the young people of today could have their freedom. And are they grateful?"

No one ever answered that question. I moved carefully to my grandfather's side and asked quietly, "Are you ill?"

He looked at me sharply. He was about to give a cutting reply, but then saw that I was sincere. "No, William," he said, "not ill."

"Then what?"

He turned and walked towards the wooden arch that the roses were woven through. I followed him into the tunnel of red Lancastrian roses and gold-flame honeysuckle. Whatever was on his mind, it was something he didn't want to share with his wife, or the rest of the family. When we were out of earshot he stopped, swung round and said, "I'm not afraid of death, boy."

"No, Grandfather."

"There is a better life than this one still to come."

"I know. The priest tells us every Sunday in church."

"That's so long as we've lived a good life in this world," he said so quietly I could barely catch the words.

"You've had a good life," I said.

He didn't reply. He was wrapped in his own thoughts and still not willing to share his true fears with one of those "idle, dishonest and weak" young people. He walked on. The scent of the golden honeysuckle was thick and sweet in my nose. So sweet and full of life that it was hard to think of Grandfather and old age and death in that late-summer garden.

"I was a soldier," he said.

"I know."

"I fought for Henry VIII against the Scots."

"A great king," I said.

The old man stopped so suddenly that I almost walked into him. "A man with blood on his hands and blood on his soul," he said and his voice was as hoarse as that crow on the tower. I was puzzled. I'd never heard him speak badly about the Tudor family before – except for Henry VIII's older daughter Mary. Bloody Mary he called her.

"I've killed men," he said.

"In battle," I put in quickly.

"Aye … and the church forgives you if you kill a man in a just fight." He looked up at me. I realized that his shrunken body had made him shorter than I was now. "Of course, the enemy think God is on their side too! He's a funny sort of God that fights on both sides, isn't he, boy?"

It was hard to believe that this withered man had been a soldier in the Scottish wars. Many was the night he had terrified us with tales of the old enemy and what would happen if they ever attacked England again.

"But … but if you fought in those battles for Henry then you must be brave," I said. "You can't be afraid to die!"

His face turned hard again. "What would you know about it?" he asked.

I stared down at the soft grass of the path, ashamed of being young.

"The man who goes into battle and says he isn't afraid is the biggest liar on God's earth," he went on fiercely. Then he seemed to remember that I was young and need-ed to learn these things. "No. It's not the fear of death that makes you sad. It's the fear of a wasted life! When you get to the gates of heaven, what are you going to say when they ask you what you've done?"

"You could tell them you fought for your king," I urged.

"But that was many, many years ago. A man can't live on the memories of what he did as a youth! No, William. If that crow has brought its message for me then I want to do one last deed before I die. One thing that you will be proud of. One thing that people will remember and talk about for as long as they live!"

"Grandfather," I said softly, "you're well over ninety years old!"

He snatched one of the faded roses from the arch at the east end of the garden. We'd walked the length of the garden and were coming back into it. He opened his hand and showed the crushed red petals that were brown and withered at the edge. "If that crow has come for me, then I don't want to be remembered like this!" He let the roses flutter and fall to the grass, and put a hand behind a blood-red rose that was vigorous and strong. "I want to be remembered like this. Do you understand, boy?"

I think I understood. If I were a bud on that bush, I could still grow to enjoy my glory. But the rose that is withered will never grow young again.

We walked back into the garden where the rest of the family looked up at us curiously. Grandfather returned their gazes, his look steadier and clearer than I ever remembered it. Even his crooked back seemed to straighten. He rested a hand on the pommel of his sword and gripped it. "I was just telling young William here about Henry VIII. The king in clothes of blood red and gold."

"A great soldier," Great-Uncle George nodded.

"But a terrible, terrible man," said Grandfather. "Have I ever told you the story of when he visited this house?" he asked.

My father gave a choking sound. "King Henry VIII!" he spluttered. "He visited this house! Marsden Hall!"

My grandfather's watery eyes sparkled with delight at his son's shocked face. "Yes, James," he repeated. "King Henry VIII visited this house – Marsden Hall."

"But ... but ..." my father began. He shook his head, bewildered. "No one has ever said anything!"

"Because it was a secret, James," Grandfather explained patiently.

"So why betray the secret now?" Grandmother asked.

"Because there are people with long memories. People on the other side of the Scottish border who remember the part the Marsdens played in their terrible defeat," my grandfather said. He was talking to the family, but looking at me. "It is important for me to tell the story before I die."

There was a stillness in the garden broken only by the soft "caw" of the black bird on the roof. "When were you thinking of dying?" Grandmother asked. "It's good of you to warn us!" Her voice was as sharp as ever, but something betrayed a shadow of fear inside her.

Grandfather looked up at the bird. "You never know," he said. "You never know when your turn will come. I want James and young William here to be prepared for the worst. I want them to know what will happen if the Scots ever cross the border and invade again. I want them to be prepared. That's why I am finally telling this secret."

"What will happen to us, Grandfather?" I asked.

He leaned forward and fixed me with a fierce stare as if he dared me to disbelieve him. "You will be the target of special assassins. Men who will seek out Marsden Hall and destroy it. Men who will tear the old house down stone by stone. Men who will look for anyone bearing the Marsden name and utterly destroy them."

Even the crow on the tower had stopped glaring down and was preening its feathers that shone in the last of the warm day's sun. Yet it seemed to be listening as carefully as the silent roses around the garden.

For a moment the spell was broken. The door to the kitchens opened and a wild-haired girl with sea-green eyes stepped out. She had come to fill the empty wine goblets that stood on the ground beside the benches. The girl's name was Meg and she knew more about the Marsden family than a servant should. Still, we trusted her, and I held out a hand, palm down, to show her she should sit and be quiet.

The girl settled on the grass and the whole family was turned towards Grandfather. Even my father settled on a bench, and he was usually as starch-stiff as his ruff.

"Tell us, Father," he said.

CHAPTER TWO

"I am in blood steeped in so far"

My grandfather rested his hands on his knees and looked around at his family. When he was sure he had everyone's attention, he began.

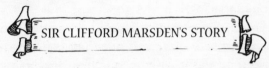

SIR CLIFFORD MARSDEN'S STORY

I was only a child when the King came to Marsden Hall. We had little warning. A troop of ten soldiers rode through our gates one evening and demanded to see my father, Sir Arthur.

They wore the green and white colours of the Tudor family with the Tudor rose on the backs of their cloaks. Their faces were as hard as their glittering breastplates and the rumble of their hooves made the ground shake under me.

I ran into the house crying, "The Scots are coming!"

That was my biggest fear. When I was misbehaving my nurse used to whisper in my ear, "A big, hairy Scotsman will come and get you and chop you up with his sword!" I spent many nights shivering under my bedclothes, hearing the old house creak and thinking it was the hairy Scotsman come to get me. I would cling to my two younger brothers and hope the hairy Scotsman would take them and leave me. Our older sister, Mary, tried to tell us it was just a story, but we didn't believe her.

When Henry's men clattered into our stable yard I was sure my time had come. I wondered what it was like to be cut into pieces. My little brothers ran to hide in the stables. Even Mary shrank away behind the great oak in the garden, while I sped into the hall.

My father was there, collecting rents from grey-faced tenants. He was about thirty years old at the time, and I remember he had his hair cut straight in the Tudor bob. Even with the log fire blazing in the hearth he needed a heavy robe in the main hall. It was before we'd had glass fitted in Marsden Hall and the house was always chilly. When I ran in crying, "The Scots are coming!", he snatched for the sword at his side, half-believing my cries. The captain of the soldiers marched through the door and I hid behind my father's great oak chair.

"Sir Arthur Marsden?" the soldier asked, speaking with a strange accent.

"Who wants to know?" my father asked, rising to his feet and pushing his chair back till I was half crushed against the wall. I didn't mind. I felt safer there. I heard the rustle of parchment being unrolled and the stranger said, "I am Captain Bevan in His Majesty King Henry VIII's service."

"Welsh," my father muttered. He seemed to be examining a document the stranger had passed to him.

The soldier went on, "I need to talk to you privately." There was a scuffling and some grumbling as he ordered the tenant farmers out of the hall. He wasn't being too gentle.

When the door closed the man walked back to my

father's table and sat down. My father sat opposite him. I hardly dared to breathe.

"The sweating sickness has come to London again," Captain Bevan said. I'd heard about the sweating sickness. Villagers said it came to Newcastle almost every summer, but we were spared it on our country estate. The victims suddenly felt ill and broke out in a heavy sweat. They could be dead in four hours. Few recovered, and the ones who did were weakened for life.

"The King is ill?" my father asked.

"No, no!" the soldier said quickly. "But he has no children – no son to take the throne if he dies. The country would be thrown into dreadful civil war like we had thirty years ago. The King's life must be preserved at all costs."

"So he's left London?"

"He's not running away, you understand. He isn't afraid. It's just that he needs to save his life for the sake of the country," the stranger explained.

"Of course," my father agreed. "So he's gone to one of his palaces in the country, has he?"

I heard the table creak as if the soldier were leaning forward to get closer to my father. He spoke very quietly. "Sir Arthur, your father fought against King Henry's father at the battle of Bosworth Field. But you have been loyal to the crown since then. We can trust you."

"Of course."

"Then I can tell you ... His Majesty is just ten miles south of here, in Durham."

My father gasped and cried, "Durham!"

"Hush, man! We don't want the world to know!"

"Sorry."

"The King has come north for a meeting so secret that thousands of lives would be lost if he were betrayed. Your own Marsden Hall would be at risk as well as the lives of everyone in Northumberland and Durham."

"A meeting in Durham?" my father asked.

"Not in Durham," the captain said and his voice was little more than a whisper. "Durham is too large a city – so is Newcastle. His Majesty plans to call together all his most loyal lords in the north of England. They would be seen and recognized if they gathered at Durham Castle. Enemy agents flock to great places like that. They would report a gathering of lords to their masters and our enemies would hear of it within a week. No, he can't meet them in Durham."

"Then where?"

"He needs a small manor house somewhere between Durham and Newcastle. A place where the King and his lords can come quietly, with no great processions and servants and armed guards and baggage. He wants to come to Marsden Hall."

My father gasped. It was as well that he did. His cry of astonishment probably hid my own.

The two men discussed the arrangements and it seemed that the King would arrive the next day at around noon. He would spend the afternoon hunting in our own Bournmoor Woods and have dinner with our family. The northern lords would arrive under the cloak of darkness and the meeting would be held that night.

"Won't people see the King arrive?" my father asked.

"He'll have very few servants with him. And you must tell everyone – your wife and your household too – that you are being visited by the King's friend, the Duke of Suffolk. No one in this area has seen either of them, so you will be believed. Henry has this new idea of being called 'Your Majesty' when his subjects speak to him. For

the sake of our secret we will go back to the old words –
call him 'Your Grace'."

The man asked to see the sleeping chambers, the stables
and the room that the King would be using, and my father
led him out of the hall. I slowly uncurled myself from
behind his chair. I found my knees were almost too weak
to hold me.

The King's visit was the most important thing that had
happened to me in my short life. But I was more interested in knowing what the great secret was. If it was going to
be hidden from enemy agents, then I felt sure that no boy
would discover it. Yet I had learned Henry's secret because
I was just a boy and no one thought I was important
enough. Even my father forgot that I had hidden behind
his chair and told me that we were to have a visit from the
Duke of Suffolk the next day!

I had never seen so much activity in Marsden Hall.
Workers were brought in from the fields and the village to
throw out the dirty rushes from the floor and replace them
with fresh ones. Extra cooks were brought into the
kitchens and Father ordered that the kitchen boys should
wear clothes, no matter how hot the kitchens became. It
seems that Henry insisted on this in his palaces.

That evening the air was heavy with smells of baking
pastries and spices. Dust rose in clouds as everything was
polished, and I watched it floating in the rays of the sun
until I was given a sharp prod by my father. "No time for
daydreaming, boy," he said. "Go to the long gallery.
There's a tailor waiting to fit you with a new coat."

I hurried along to the gallery where portraits of the
Marsden family looked down gloomily. Grandfather
Anthony Marsden was my favourite. He'd fought for King
Richard III and then joined the victor, Henry VII, to turn

back a Scottish invasion. I always hoped that one day I would follow the same road and become a hero. Something about the Marsden habit of remembering old stories makes us all like that.

I found my brothers being measured for new clothes and my sister being taught how to wait on Queen Catherine. She showed me her curtsey, which was so low her long hair brushed the floor. Mary usually made do with a bob and a nod of the head. My coat was in the dark red of the Marsden family colours and my brothers were having tiny uniforms made to match.

That night we scarcely slept in the wide bed we shared; my brothers were asking questions about this Duke of Suffolk – questions I couldn't answer. We fell asleep shortly before dawn, but I was out of bed when the first blood-red rays of the sun crept through the shutters of my room.

My father was already up and ordering the household while my mother was organizing the servants. "Clifford," she said when she caught sight of me, "it is usual for the eldest son of the house to be the chief guest's cupbearer. You will wait on the Duke of Suffolk himself."

"Isn't the King the chief guest?" I asked.

My mother frowned. "The King? Why would the King come to Marsden Hall?" she asked.

I felt my face burn with shame and confusion. The King wasn't here yet and I'd already betrayed him. "I meant … I meant to say …" I stammered. Then the steward, John Johnston, arrived with a question about wine and I was saved. The steward was given the task of showing me how to serve the Duke of Suffolk's wine. Finally he sat at the head of the table, pretended to be the chief guest, and invited me to serve him.

My hand trembled as I lifted the jug that was too heavy for my small arm. I tried to tilt it, but had to use my other hand to tip it further. I watched in horror as the wine missed the cup and splashed over the stone-faced steward's white linen shirt. My brothers giggled and thought it was fine sport to watch me struggle in this way.

"We will have to hope that you don't do that at tonight's dinner," John Johnston said. He made me practise over and over again until I'd mastered the skill, then taught me where to stand, how to bow and how to ask if the guest wanted more wine.

The thought of spilling wine over the King terrified me. I knew that I would soak him and that he would have me executed on the spot. I did think that I might lean over the minstrels' gallery, let myself slip over and break my arms. In fact I wouldn't have minded if I'd broken my neck. But I hadn't the courage to do it. I'd just have to pour wine on the King and let him execute me. The secret I shared with my father was too much for a child to bear alone. It was the most miserable morning of my life.

But when the sundial over the door showed noon and the King's party rode in I forgot all my fears. My tutor had told me legends from Ancient Greece and I'd heard about the gods on Mount Olympus. When I first set eyes on King Henry VIII, I'll swear I believed he was one of those gods come down to earth. Perhaps my childish mind was right – for the gods were wonderfully beautiful, but utterly cruel and selfish. And so was Henry.

That afternoon he was wearing plain green hunting clothes. I was disappointed to see that he was not wearing his crown. But as he jumped down from his horse I saw that he was a giant of a young man. And it wasn't just looking up at him as a child that made him seem so huge. It was a simple fact; Henry was the tallest man I have ever met – six foot three inches or more.

The king had red-gold hair and rose-coloured skin as fine as any woman's. His bright blue eyes were fierce and restless. I know now that they were just a little too close together and that his soft mouth was just a little too small under the neat red beard. But when I first saw him I thought he was the handsomest man in the world.

The family stood in a line to welcome him. He ignored Mary and stood in front of me and my brothers.

"Who are the boys?" he asked suddenly.

My father placed an arm around my shoulders and pushed me forward a pace. "My sons, Clifford, John and Simon, Your Grace," he said.

The King stepped forward, placed a hand under my chin and lifted my face. There was a brief flash of pain and envy in those ice-blue eyes before he said, "You are blessed, Sir Arthur. A son! Three sons! What I wouldn't give to have just one."

"We pray that you will one day," my father said.

"Your prayers are welcome," the King said. "I did have one son, but he died young," he added bitterly. Suddenly he smiled, turned and looked towards the horses that stood patiently behind him. For the first time I saw the woman who was with him. "But we will have a son one day soon, won't we?" he said.

The woman was in a plain hunting dress too. She looked a little older than the King and had none of his energy. Even the red-gold hair looked duller than Henry's, and her pale face was round and plain, and set in a worried frown. I found it hard to believe that this was his queen, Catherine of Aragon, but when she spoke I heard her

Spanish accent. "You will have your son, Your Grace," she said with a meek bow of the head.

"Now, Marsden," Henry cried, "show me these woods that I've heard so much about. Good deer, is that right?"

"Fine fat ones, Your Grace," my father said proudly. He led the way to the stables and kennels so that the King could choose a fresh horse and inspect the hounds. An hour later a small group set off to Bournmoor Woods, the hounds baying loud enough to frighten every deer in the county. My father led the way and the Queen rode alongside her husband. She looked almost happy.

Of course I stayed behind and worked alongside my mother and the steward to prepare the tables in the hall for the King's supper. Fish were brought in from Wearmouth, and a freshly killed swan from the River Wear. Our precious silver goblets, spoons and saltcellar were brought out and polished. Steward John Johnston made a great show of placing the huge white tablecloth on the top table, folding napkins to make models of animals or birds, and setting finger bowls ready to be filled with fresh rosewater.

My mother was hurrying between the pantry and the kitchen and the hall. "You will eat a little before you wait on His Grace," she told us.

"Yes, Mother," Mary said, practising her low curtsey.

"And remember, no spitting, no wiping your nose on your sleeve and no scratching yourself," she said to me and my brothers.

"No, Mother."

"And keep your thumb out of his wine goblet and don't speak unless he speaks to you," she said to me.

"Yes, Mother," I said. My fear of spilling the wine was

replaced by a sort of dazed tiredness, long before it was time to dine.

As the sun began to set I heard the howling of the hounds as they returned, and soon afterwards the King himself threw open the door. His pale skin was glowing pink and his small eyes were glittering with pleasure. Across each shoulder he had a fine deer which he carried as lightly as if they were lambs.

He threw them on the floor at my mother's feet and bowed low, sweeping off his hat. "Your supper, my lady," he said.

Queen Catherine followed him in, looking truly pleased for the first time since she had arrived. She looked down happily on the bloodsoaked animals and said, "His Grace is a fine hunter, is he not?"

"Steward!" Henry cried. "Have these animals skinned. Put them on a spit over the fire while I change. We'll eat in an hour."

Steward John Johnston's mouth fell open and he tried to find the right words. "They will scarcely be cooked in an hour, Your Grace."

The King shrugged and laughed, baring his fine teeth. "No matter. I like the taste of blood!" he said, and allowed my mother to lead him and the Queen to their chambers.

The deer were skinned and set to roast in the deep fireplace at the end of the hall. One of the kitchen boys stood beside the fire and kept the meat turning, all the while complaining because he had to wear his shirt although he was half-roasting himself.

The tables were laid with more food than I'd ever seen: cheeses and pies and pastries and prune tarts and eggs, all with bowls of sauces and spices. The swan was brought in, roasted, but dressed again in its feathers and with the long neck. Its dull eyes stared at me.

Jugglers, dancers and musicians had arrived from Newcastle and were practising in the horseshoe space between the tables. At last the steward called for silence, and the King walked into the hall with the Queen a step behind him.

She shone like some pale, fine moon in a silk dress with black Spanish lace. But her radiance was dimmed by the King, who was as bright as the sun. His velvet doublet was as red as the blood of the deer and his collar was heavy with gold. Diamonds the size of walnuts dripped from the collar and heavy rings shimmered on every finger and thumb. He sat at the table on a low platform at the end of our hall, with the Queen and my mother on either side of him. My father and Captain Bevan sat at each end of the table. The feast began.

I moved between the gleaming couple with my wine flagon, so numbed by the majesty of the man that I didn't tremble in the slightest. I filled his wine glass over and over again without spilling a drop. I watched with awe as he placed huge handfuls of food in his mouth and waited in horror for the blood running down his chin to drip on to the marvellous scarlet doublet. But the blood seemed to soak into his fine beard and he wiped it away with the back of his hand.

The King talked loudly between filling his mouth, in a voice that seemed too high for such a large man. And he laughed a lot and cheered for the performers who pleased him.

After what must have been at least two hours he rose to his feet, stretched and belched. This was a sign that the feast was over. Our guests from local manors rose too and hastened away into the night. They seemed to know that they were not welcome for what was to follow.

Henry told Captain Bevan to make sure the dancers and jugglers were well away from the hall before our noble guests started to arrive, and the officer hurried off to order his bodyguard to take rush torches and check that the grounds of Marsden Hall were not being watched by strangers.

I was told to stay in attendance on the King, and so I was there for the most secret meeting.

The King turned to my father and said, "Now we are alone, Marsden, I think I can tell you the reason we are here."

"If His Majesty wishes," my father said.

"His Majesty wishes," said Henry, smiling slowly, "His Majesty wishes to go to war with France."

My father stiffened for a brief moment. Then he said, "Ah," as if he understood everything. But I was only a child. And I understood nothing.

Chapter Three

"I have supped full with horrors"

The family looked towards the old house as if they were seeing it for the first time.

"King Henry? Stayed here?" my father said. "Who'd have believed it! What an honour."

My grandfather pulled his thin lips down at the corners. "What a curse," he said.

"What do you mean?" said my father.

"I was a child at the time," said Grandfather. "I didn't understand what a French war would mean to the Marsdens. But you are old enough to see where it could lead," he said sharply.

Grandmother would argue that a rose was red if Grandfather said it was white. She sniffed and said, "France is a long way from the north of England. When we go to war with France, we pay a few more taxes, we send a few men from the fields to fight."

Grandfather turned his beaky nose towards her. "If that's what you think, then you're wrong," he said.

"Wrong? I can't remember the last time I was wrong!" Grandmother cackled.

My mother could see an argument brewing and put in a few words to turn aside the storm. "It's the Scots you're thinking of, isn't it?"

The old man gave a sharp nod of his bird head and said, "Exactly! The Scots have been our enemies for hundreds of years. They've always believed that Northumberland should be theirs in fact in the days of the first Henry, the Scottish border did come down to the Tyne, just ten miles north of here. Oh, we've pushed them back to Berwick since then, but they've never forgotten and never forgiven us."

"And they take every chance they can to attack us again," my mother said.

"Exactly! The Scots have always been good friends of the French. If England goes to war with Scotland, then the French will help by attacking England ..."

"I see!" I interrupted. "So when Henry VIII said he was going to war with France, the Scots would invade the north of England."

"Good boy," Grandfather said. "And all those years ago, when I was a boy, Marsden Hall became the meeting place for all Henry's captains as they plotted to destroy the Scots. The Scots haven't forgotten that either. If they ever march through Northumberland again, they would march that extra ten miles to have the pleasure of destroying Marsden Hall and everyone bearing the Marsden name."

The family went silent as we thought about this. "When the Queen dies," my mother said slowly, "there is a chance that James VI will come from Scotland and take her throne. They even say the English lords will invite him. What will happen to us then?"

"A bloodless invasion," Grandfather said. "The Scots will come south and be our lords after all this time. There is every chance that the ones with the long memories will do as much damage to Marsden Manor as they can."

My father looked irritated and snapped, "What can we do about it?"

Grandfather spread his hands wide, but, before he could reply, Grandmother said, "Pray that good Queen Elizabeth lives forever!"

"Or learn how to fight," Meg said. Since my mother had saved the girl from the poor house and given her a job in the kitchens, she had found herself a new family. The Marsden family. No one, except Father, seemed to mind too much when she joined us to listen to family tales. "If the Scots came here killing Marsdens, I'd skin them with my kitchen knife."

"Thank you, Meg, but we hope it won't come to that," my mother said. The girl looked almost disappointed that she wouldn't be let loose on an attacking army. For a moment I felt sorry for the first Scottish soldier to set foot in Marsden Manor.

Meg's ideas were forgotten when a young man came into the garden from the stable yard. We turned to look at him. He was a wonderful sight: dressed in the latest fashion with a doublet of silk in bright peacock green, slashed to show a pink lining. His snowy ruff was wide and frilled with lace and his soft green cap hung at a wild angle on his long fair hair. His beard was so fine it was almost invisible on his smooth, round face.

"Have I the pleasure of addressing Sir James Marsden?" he asked Grandfather.

"I'm Sir James," Father said gruffly. His nostrils widened to take in the flowery scent that hung around the young visitor.

"I am so glad to have found you!" the young man cried. "I am Hugh Richmond in the service of Lord Lambton. Those woods are so dark!"

Grandmother gave a huge sniff and murmured, "I didn't know Lord Lambton had a zoo. Someone should tell him a peacock has escaped!"

Either the young man didn't hear, or he pretended not to. "His lordship requests that you join him tomorrow, Sir James. The traitor who called himself Humphrey Vere goes to trial in York Castle next week and you are needed to give evidence."

My father raised his chin and inflated his chest. "Since I arrested the villain it is natural that I should attend his trial," he said. Meg looked as if she were going to argue. The truth is that she had as much to do with his arrest as anyone.

"Bring our visitor some wine," my mother said quickly. "Sit down, Master Richmond. You've ridden all the way from Lambton?"

"Five miles if it's a yard!" he replied, falling on to the seat like a sack of flour on to the floor of the mill. "And those woods! So dark!"

"So you said," Grandmother put in. "Afraid of the dark, are you?"

"But of course!" the man gasped. "I couldn't see where I was going. I might have torn my jacket on a briar bush."

Grandmother threw back her head and laughed. "There are worse things in Bournmoor Woods than briar bushes," she said.

"Worse?"

"Ghosts."

He thought about this for a few moments. "Well, to be honest, I'd rather meet a ghost than a bramble bush any day. This doublet cost me five guineas from a London tailor!"

Even Grandfather was smiling now, and the young man

seemed to enjoy it. When Meg came out with his wine, she stopped in the doorway. "Supper is ready," she said. "Will our guest be joining us?"

"He will, I'm sure," my mother said. "And he'll stay the night, won't you, Master Richmond? It will save you going back through the woods."

The man smiled gratefully and followed her into the house. He kept us entertained with stories about the people in the Queen's court in London and the castles in the south of England. The stories were not much more than gossip, but he was amusing and made us laugh as we gathered round the huge old fireplace after a supper of mutton in beer followed by pears in syrup.

"King Henry VIII ate venison from a deer that was cooked over this fire," my father boasted.

Grandfather looked annoyed. After all, it was his story.

"Really?" Hugh Richmond said. "I didn't know he came this far north!"

"It was a secret visit," Grandfather said quickly. "He met his northern lords here to tell them that he was going to war with the French and they would have to guard against a Scottish invasion."

"This is the closest I've ever been to Scotland," Hugh said with a shudder, "and the closest I'd ever want to go if I had my way."

"The Borders are quiet compared with when Henry was here," Grandfather said.

"Did you see him yourself?" Hugh Richmond asked.

"I did. I served his wine. He slept upstairs in the East Wing – why, you could sleep there yourself, Master Richmond, if you wish!"

Lord Lambton's messenger was pleased at the thought and mother sent the steward to prepare the room and warm the sheets with a warming pan. Hugh turned to Grandfather. "So did the Scots invade?"

Grandfather held his hands up to the fire and seemed to see pictures of the past in the flames. "King James IV was on the throne of Scotland at the time. Of course, he was married to Henry VIII's sister, Margaret, so there should have been peace between the kingdoms. But the hatred, Master Hugh, the hatred. A brother and sister on the thrones can't make people forget their history. I sometimes think the Scots are born to hate the English."

"Dreadful people, the Scots," Hugh said.

"I always thought that," Grandfather said. "Then I remember the things that the English have done to them – the things I did myself – and I wonder if maybe we deserve their hatred."

"We fought to defend our country," my father said stiffly.

Grandfather didn't disagree, but he went on. "Kings like Henry VIII didn't simply want to defeat the Scots and keep them over the border. He wanted to crush them and enslave them. When he marched north his armies put whole villages to the sword. It didn't matter if they came upon a castle or a cottage, they burned it. The crops were destroyed so the people couldn't survive in the Borders. Their cattle and sheep were slaughtered to feed the English armies. And they didn't care if they killed Scottish soldiers, or unarmed farmers and their wives and children. It wasn't war, it was butchery."

"The Scots did the same to the English," Father argued angrily. "No one with any sense would choose to live in Northumberland. It's a wasteland. Folk who try to scratch a living can build up their farms only to have them raided and robbed by the Scottish Reivers."

"What are the Reivers?" Hugh asked me quietly.

"Cattle thieves," I said. He nodded and looked at Grandfather.

"Aye, and the Scottish farmers are robbed by the English Reivers. Backwards and forwards. Endless war. The Queen's law doesn't mean a thing in the Borders." He turned to our guest. "You can see what we fear. What will happen if James VI takes the English throne?"

Hugh Richmond wasn't allowed to answer. "Nothing will stop them," Father said. "Nothing."

It was the same gloomy talk we'd had a hundred times, and no one had an answer. "Our guest doesn't want to hear about Scottish threats," Great-Uncle George said. "Tell him about the time we beat them! Tell him about Flodden Field!" he said, smacking his lips noisily at the thought.

"Ah, yes, Flodden," Grandfather said. "I was telling the family about Henry VIII's war against France when you arrived. They planned the defence against the Scots in this very room," he said, and the ghosts of the long-dead lords seemed to linger in the deep brown shadows of the rafters.

CHAPTER FOUR

"So foul and fair a day I have not seen."

SIR CLIFFORD MARSDEN'S STORY

Henry was young and Henry was a knight. He wanted to fight someone just to prove his strength. England had once ruled part of France and Henry took it into his wild young mind to get it back again. He would lead a brilliant crusade with all the colour and glory of charging knights, streaming banners, crumbling castles and untold treasures. He didn't see real war where men die slow, cruel, muddy deaths, and disease and starvation kill far more than any sword. He was young.

Now Henry knew that as soon as he left England, King James IV of Scotland would invade up in the north. So he gathered his army to set sail for France, but left another army up here to deal with the Scots. And who was his commander while he was away? He left his queen, Catherine of Aragon, in charge.

That may surprise you, but remember I had seen her eyes shine with the pleasure of the hunt and the joy she took in seeing the bleeding deer – the deer that lay just where we are sitting now. She was a woman, but she had the stomach for a fight against James.

Catherine did not go into battle, you understand. The commander in the north was the loyal Earl of Surrey. As armed men gathered from all over the north of England, so they gathered north of the border.

Queen Margaret of Scotland was desperately unhappy – her husband was going to war against her brother. First she begged James not to fight, but the King refused. And then he had a ghostly visitor.

Of course we all believe in ghosts, shades of the dead who appear with warnings. Well, James went to the chapel in his palace at Linlithgow that summer, surrounded by his lords. As he knelt in silent prayer the church door opened. Every man there fixed his eyes on the strange figure who stood in the doorway: a man in a blue gown with a linen belt, with hair down to his shoulders and a high, bald forehead. He was a ghastly, pale man of about fifty, and he carried a pikestaff in his hand. He stepped forward and said, "I would speak with the King!"

The lords were terrified and parted to let the strange man see the King. Then the figure spoke. "Sir, I am sent to warn you not to go where you plan. If you do, then you will not do well, and the people with you will suffer."

The figure vanished like the whip of a whirlwind and was seen no more. Sir David Lindsay and Sir John Inglis who were standing by the King reached forward to grab the man and question him, but even though he was standing between them, they could not lay a hand on him before he vanished.

Now, some people have said that this was a trick that Queen Margaret arranged to stop her husband from invading England. But if it was, no one can say how it was arranged. What's more, it failed. James vowed to go on.

He gathered his army in Edinburgh. Or should I say his

three armies! For he had his knights on horseback and their men in steel caps and chain mail. They would be fighting with their long pikes, three times the height of a man.

The second army were the Lowlanders, the men from Edinburgh and the Borders. They knew the English well and robbed them whenever they had the chance. You could tell them because of their woollen trousers and their sheepskin jackets. If they wore any protection at all, it was a boiled leather jerkin. They carried the long pike too.

But the third army was the strangest – they were the Highlanders. They wore something like a thick wool shirt down to the knees, and they stood out on the battlefield because they dyed their shirts a shade of yellow. They were brave fighters, good archers and terrifying with their double-handed swords. But they didn't like long wars. They went to a battle, fought and looted cattle and sheep, then went back home to their Highlands. James was going to have trouble with them.

It was one of the largest armies ever gathered against England. And James had his great brass cannon brought from Stirling and Edinburgh Castles – twenty-two in all and each one pulled by thirty-two oxen and each with a team of workmen to smooth the road and fill in the muddy holes along the way to England.

Still, the army was cursed. On the night before they set off from Edinburgh there was a terrible cry heard in the Market Place. A loud voice wailed out the names of the lords and knights who would die in the war. No one knew if the voice was a human's or a spirit's, but the dreadful truth is that the men who were named never came back.

It was around this time of the year – early September – and Marsden Manor was caught up with the excitement and the thrill of the coming battle. Spies were hurrying through with news of over sixty thousand Scotsmen marching towards us. My father took out his armour and oiled it, and had the best tenants of Marsden Manor fitted with chain mail and wool cloaks. There were twenty-one in all. Our steward, John Johnston, was father's sergeant and I still remember how fine he looked in the dark-red cloak with the embroidered silver badge of the Marsden family – the badge that shows Saint George slaying the dragon.

They gathered on the village green, and everyone took a day from their work in the fields to cheer them on their way. They carried much shorter pikes than the Scots – axe-edged weapons they called "billhooks" – and the cold steel shone in the September sun. An ox-cart was loaded with spare weapons, tents and blankets, food and cooking pots.

One of the boys carried a drum and another played a pipe. When they struck up a marching tune I could feel the blood racing through my body till I thought I'd burst. My father was the only one on a horse. He leaned down to kiss my mother and Mary. Then Mother lifted up me and my brothers so he could kiss us too. I can still remember the smell of oil and steel and leather.

"Look after your mother, Clifford," he said. I thought it a strange thing to say, but I nodded.

"Why are you crying, Mother?" I asked. She didn't answer.

I was young, you see. I didn't understand. I thought they would go and drive the Scots back over the border, then return home in triumph. I just never thought that they could die. I never thought that fewer than twenty-one would come back home.

John Johnston arranged the men in twos, and they marched off north to the rattling beat of the drum. Everyone in the village ran after them and followed until they reached the main road to Newcastle. I'd never seen so many happy people. It all seemed such a mighty adventure.

The Marsden road joined the Newcastle road two miles north of the manor. That's where our troops met the other groups of men from the south, each with their own badges and cloaks and banners and shields. The colours were like flowers in a summer field. Poppy reds and cornflower blues mingled with leaf greens and vetch purples. The Durham men marched behind the ancient banner of Saint Cuthbert, a red cross on a white background with red roses round the outside. "But the Marsden reds are the smartest, aren't they, Mother?" I shouted over the beating drums, the drumming feet and the rising wind that made the banners snap. And still she couldn't answer. She clung on to Mary's arm looking pale and afraid, while my brothers danced and leapt to the beat of the drums and pretended to fight one another with pieces of twisted straw for swords.

My father turned and looked back one last time. I could see him over the heads of the Marsden troop. He raised a hand and I watched him till he was lost in the distant crowds. "They say we'll have thirty thousand men by the time we reach the Scots!" one of the marchers cried cheerfully. I felt sorry for him because his uniform was black and dull. I didn't know that soon I'd be wearing midnight black myself.

The marching line seemed to stretch forever. Over six thousand from Lancashire, led by Sir Edward Stanley. "That's who'll be commanding your father," one of the farmers said to me, pointing to the knight on a dark bay horse.

It was late by the time we got back home to Marsden Hall. The sun had not quite set, but the sky was deep purple with storm clouds that were rolling over the distant Pennine hills. Crows were flocking back to their nests in Bournmoor Woods after a day in the fields. Most were blown across the sky like tattered funeral clothes, but one battled against the storm to circle three times round the west tower of the house before settling there. A dark-haired young girl ran past crying, "That's bad luck, that is!" She was a strange village child called Jane Fell. She ran off before I could ask her what she meant.

That night my brothers sank into our bed, exhausted from the excitement, but I took a long time to get to sleep. Over the rattling of the shutters I could hear the people singing at the village tavern long after dark. And, when they finally went quiet, I could hear my mother sobbing softly when the wind dropped for a moment. I fell asleep at last and dreamed of marching in a deep rose-red cloak against the men in the yellow shirts.

They were only away two or three weeks. The news was little more than gossip at first. Then, at last, a soldier in the King's green and white stopped for a fresh horse and gave us the news. "We met them at a place called Flodden and we smashed them!"

"And our men?"

The man was dust-stained and tired. He just shrugged. "There were at least ten thousand Scots to bury and only a thousand or so of our English, so your men will be safe enough, don't worry."

Two days later troops of men began appearing on the Newcastle road, marching back south towards Durham.

The fine uniforms were stained and worn, some blood-soaked and some torn. The men were marching more slowly and wearily than they had when they left just three weeks before. They should have been happy. I didn't understand the shadows that lurked behind their tired eyes. I've seen those shadows a hundred times since. They are the ghosts of the men they have killed and the friends they have watched dying on the red-stained grass.

The next day I was in the garden, playing with my brothers, when I heard the noise of shouting from the village. A village woman who sometimes did washing for us raced into the rose-covered archway and cried, "The Marsden men are back, my lady! They've just turned off the Newcastle road!"

I turned to hurry after her, but my mother grabbed my hand and made me walk quietly by her side. The young ones were left in the care of Mary. I suddenly felt special and important.

The men trooped quietly behind the ox-cart, their heads bowed and the deep-rose cloaks stained with mud. There was no drum, no pipe and, I realized, no man on a horse leading them. The men walked past us, no longer marching in step. They looked up at my mother and me with pity and pain on their weathered faces.

The ox-cart that had held sacks full of flour now held the empty sacks. And the sacks were laid over the floor of the cart, covering something the shape and size of a man. The excitement of the villagers had suddenly died the way a lark's song dies as it drops from the sky. The chief tenants mingled with the returning soldiers; their wives and children joined them and followed the cart. As they passed us they stopped one at a time and bowed their heads to me the way they had done to my father. Some knelt quickly, took my hand and kissed it. My mother took my hand, and we turned and followed them to the gates of Marsden Hall.

With no orders spoken the cart stopped and four men lifted out their lifeless bundle and carried it into the hall. Steward Johnston stepped forward. He seemed so much older than when he had left Marsden Manor just a few weeks before. "The women of the village will lay him out," he said.

"Thank you," my mother whispered. Then she added, "Were you there, Johnston?"

"Yes, madam."

"Will you tell us about it?"

"Of course."

It was my first taste of grief, but I didn't feel a thing. Nothing at all. Tears, regrets and anger came later.

My mother made sure Johnston had food and wine after his march. Then she sat down in her chair by the fire. I moved to sit on the stool at her feet, but she shook her head and pointed to my father's chair. I sat in it for the first time. My feet didn't reach the floor.

Johnston sat at the opposite side of the hearth and began to speak in a flat voice. "The Scots crossed the border and took the castles at Wark, Etal and Ford. Then they stopped and waited. They chose their high ground at a place called Flodden. They were hoping that the further we had to march the more tired we would be."

"And the closer they stayed to their supplies in Scotland," my mother said. "Arthur said they would do that."

"We reached them on September the eighth," the steward went on. "They sat on Flodden Hill and watched us march across the muddy valley below them. The weather had been stormy for the week before and the low land was flooded. The Earl of Surrey sent a message to King James and challenged him to meet us on the low ground. James refused. He said that an earl couldn't tell a king what to do."

"A proud man," my mother said. "And the Bible tells us, 'Pride goeth before destruction, and an haughty spirit before a fall'."

"Indeed, madam. If King James had come to fight us on level ground, his huge army might have trampled us into the marsh. Of course a lot of the Highlanders had looted the cattle and sheep and gone off to their homes. They say they took the sweating sickness with them from Edinburgh and that killed more. It was still a mighty army. Yet James chose to stay on his hill."

"You attacked him up the hill?" I asked in my piping voice. Even at that young age I knew it was a dangerous and bold thing to do. I'd heard the tales of ancient battles from my father.

"The Earl of Surrey was too wise for that, sire," Johnston replied. It was the first time he'd called me "sire". "Instead he marched on north to Scotland, then swung round behind James. The Scots guns were pointing the wrong way, of course. We were meeting them the way we wanted, Scottish pikes against English billhooks."

"Their pikes are so much longer," my mother said.

"But clumsy to use. The Scots stand in a dense block and rest the pikes on the shoulders of the man in front. When that man falls then another steps forward. It is a good defence against charging horsemen, but our billhooks can chop through the pike handles and we can swing them at the enemy," Johnston explained.

"The Marsden men were chosen by the Earl of Surrey to fight with my lord Stanley. And it was Stanley who led the attack on the side of the Scottish pikemen. They saw us coming. They tried to turn, but they were too slow. We hit them with our billhooks and cut them down like corn till we slipped in the blood on the grass."

"And Sir Arthur?" my mother asked.

"He was on horseback so we could see him to follow him. But our leaders on horseback were the targets for every Scottish bowman. Sir Arthur halted us before the attack and said, 'You are fighting for your king, but you are also fighting for Marsden Manor. These Scots will be your masters if you don't stop them now. Give your all. Give your life if need be.' Then he drew his sword and signalled for us to advance."

John Johnston stopped and looked at the soot-stained rushes at his feet. "Go on," my mother said.

"The horse was brought down," Johnston said and his voice was choked. "Your husband landed on his feet, swinging his sword. But ... but he was surrounded by Highlanders in their yellow shirts. He disappeared before we could get to him."

"Thank you, Johnston," my mother said.

"The battle didn't start till four o'clock," the man went on. "It was dark by the time we'd finished. We weren't even sure who had won till we went over the battlefield next day. We found your husband that next morning."

"But the English did win?"

"There were twelve thousand dead Scots – including King James," said the steward.

"Poor Queen Margaret," my mother sighed.

"She's the enemy!" I cried.

My mother looked down at me with sad eyes. "She's a mother with a baby son and a dead husband," she said simply. "I know how she feels."

"Your husband died a hero," Johnston said.

My mother lifted me down from my father's chair. "Come, Clifford. We must find you some black clothes to wear."

CHAPTER FIVE

"Peep through the blanket of the dark"

My grandfather looked at the solemn group who sat around the same fireplace where he'd heard the steward's story so many years before.

"I'm sorry, sir," our visitor Hugh Richmond said. His bright clothes shone in the light of the fire and seemed unsuited to the tragic tale of my great-grandfather's death.

Grandfather sighed. "The loss of a father was sad," he said. "I'd become lord of Marsden Manor while I was still a child. But the really sad thing was the way it changed my life. I was no longer afraid of the stories of the hairy Scotsman coming to cut me into pieces. Instead I wanted him to come. I hated him, I wanted to fight him, and I wanted revenge. I spent the next fifty years looking for that revenge! I wasted my life with my heart burning with hatred."

"King Henry must have been delighted with his men," Hugh said.

Grandfather looked at him steadily. "Now that's the strange thing. He was not pleased. He was not pleased at all. For a start, the Earl of Surrey defeated James at Flodden, then turned back home. He'd saved us from the invasion, his job was done. He couldn't follow the Scots back over the border because he didn't have enough supplies for his men. Henry said Surrey should have followed the Scots and destroyed them. He hated the Scots as passionately as any man alive, and he spent the rest of his life trying to destroy them."

"He had King James out of the way," Hugh argued.

"And said he was sad to lose his brother-in-law."

My mother put her needlework on her knee and said, "At least he must have been pleased with his poor queen? He'd left her in command."

Grandfather raised a bony finger and said, "That is the strangest tale of all. The Earl of Surrey brought James's body to be buried in England and took the dead King's surcoat to Queen Catherine. It was a fine cloth with gold edging, and it was deeply stained with the blood of King James. Catherine was delighted. She sent the coat across to France where Henry was still fighting. And do you think he was pleased? He was furious! Henry was the King of England and wanted to be the greatest king in Europe. He wanted every ounce of glory for himself. His queen's victory was almost too much for him to bear."

"He was jealous," Grandmother said. "Just like a man."

Grandfather had to agree for once. "He was jealous. Catherine had failed to give him the sons he wanted and now she had outshone him in war. He never forgave her. In the end, of course, he divorced her, and look at the trouble that has caused us ever since."

"And all for the sake of a bloodstained coat," my mother said.

"Sir Clifford," Hugh said to my grandfather, "you said that after Flodden you spent fifty years looking for revenge. Did you get it?"

"There are half a million Scots," the old man said, with a harsh laugh. "How many would I have to kill to get that revenge? Ten? Or a hundred? Or every last one? And, don't forget, there were twelve thousand Scots who died and left fatherless children up there! They would be just as happy to see me dead! No wonder they hate us so much. Now I'm old and close to death myself ..."

"Don't say that!" Grandmother said sharply.

"Old and close to death myself," the old man repeated, "I'd like to find another way to put an end to all this hatred. One last good deed before I die."

My father rose to his feet, stretched and yawned loudly. "You must excuse me, Master Richmond. If I'm to be on the road tomorrow I need my sleep. If I'm to put a rope around a plotting traitor's neck, then I want to be fit to enjoy it," he added savagely, looking at my grandfather with some disgust.

That was the signal for the evening talk to end and for us all to go to bed. I was undressing when Meg knocked on the door and came in quickly, closing the door behind her. "I've brought you a warming pan made with fresh ashes from the fire."

"Thanks, Meg," I said.

In the light of my wax candle her sea-green eyes looked deep and dark and fierce. "The old man's growing soft towards the Scots, then," she said. "When you become lord of Marsden Manor you won't let them destroy us, will you?"

The truth was I didn't know what I'd do. "I won't let them destroy you," I said. She looked pleased.

"We trust you, Master William," she said.

"Thanks," I said weakly.

"When the old Queen dies they'll come and get us," she said.

"Perhaps."

"But you'll fight like old Sir Arthur, won't you?"

"Yes," I said. That was always the answer. Fight and fight again.

She stood awkwardly at the foot of the bed. Then she seemed to make up her mind and spoke in a rush. "I think that Hugh Richmond is up to something."

I blinked. "What?"

"Up to something!"

"What thing?"

"No good."

"What sort of no good?"

"I don't know what sort of no good, or I'd stop him," she said breathlessly.

"Then ... then why do you suspect him?" I asked.

She sat down firmly on the end of the bed and spoke in a low voice. "The servants helped him unpack his horse, and he had lots of letters and weapons and spare clothes and food in his saddle packs."

"So what?" I asked.

"So he is supposed to be bringing a message from Lambton Castle five miles away. Why does he have enough supplies to get him to London and back?"

"I don't know," I sighed. "You know I'm just a stupid man. I'm sure you are going to tell me just what he's up to. You're usually right."

She smiled smugly. "I don't think you're a stupid man," she said. "I think you're a stupid boy. But, since you're desperate to know what I think, I'll tell you."

"That'll be entertaining," I said.

"Don't mock me, William," she said.

I coughed in apology. "A small joke, Meg."

She bounced to her feet, then sat down again next to me. "I was watching him listening to your grandfather. He was ever so interested in the story."

"It was a good story."

"But he was watching your grandfather too carefully. He seemed to be planning something."

"And you can tell me what he's planning," I said.

"Murder."

"What!"

"Keep your voice down, or he'll come in here and murder us first."

"Meg, will you talk sense. Why would he want to murder Grandfather?"

"Revenge."

"Revenge?"

"You heard what your grandfather said about revenge. It just goes on and on. The old man did a lot of cruel deeds in Scotland. They haven't forgotten. They've sent Hugh Richmond to assassinate him. The Lambton Castle story is just a lie. He wanted to get into the house, stay the night, then creep along to your grandfather's room and murder him. Then he'll take his horse and flee over the border to his home in Scotland."

"What makes you think he's a Scot?"

"Hugh is a Scots name," she said with a look of triumph.

"But Richmond is a town in Yorkshire," I pointed out.

"He could have lied about being called Richmond."

"Then why didn't he lie about being called Hugh?"

"Keep your voice down."

"Why didn't he lie about being called Hugh?" I hissed.

She chewed savagely on her finger end. "I don't know," she finally admitted. "But if I'm right, and if your grandfather wakes up dead tomorrow morning, then you'll be sorry."

"Not as sorry as Grandfather," I snapped.

"So? Are you going to do something?"

"What do you suggest?" I asked.

"Keep a watch on your grandfather's room. Guard him for the night."

I was tired. I wanted to stretch out on my bed and sleep for a week. "You can do it," I said.

"We need two of us to take turns in staying awake." She had an answer for nearly everything.

"I sleep first," I said.

"Agreed," she said with a suddenly bright smile. I wondered how anyone other than an owl or a bat could be that awake at midnight. She opened the heavy oak door to my room and looked down the corridor. I blew out my candle and lay, still dressed, on top of my bed.

I think I had fallen asleep and was dreaming of being attacked by an army of yellow-shirted warriors. The more I tried to run the more my feet slipped on the bloodsoaked grass. They ran after me, hands reaching out to drag me down. I wriggled away, but I felt it, I felt the sharp-nailed claw gripping me like an eagle. I gave a groan of despair and woke.

"William!" she was saying. "William! Wake up." Her strong hand was gripping my shoulder.

"Woz? Uh? Woz ... who?"

"Hush! Just look!"

I sat up. My bedroom door was open. My room was in darkness. The corridor beyond should have been equally dark, but a yellow flicker was lighting the dark panels of the wall. Floorboards creaked.

Someone was walking along the corridor and trying to do it on tiptoe.

"I told you!" Meg whispered. "He's come to cut your grandfather's throat!"

CHAPTER SIX

"Methought I heard a voice cry, 'Sleep no more!'"

I wasn't sure if I was suffering a nightmare, or if Meg was really there in my room. I sat up. I heard a soft tap on a door along the corridor. It seemed to be Grandfather's room.

"Murderers don't knock on the door to warn their victims," I told Meg.

"They do if they haven't got a key," she retorted.

I struggled to my feet, took a step towards my door, collided with Meg and clung to her to stop myself falling. We staggered towards the candle-shadows like two wrestlers and collided with the door post.

The man in the corridor looked up. He seemed more frightened than we were. "Ooh! It's you."

"Yes," Meg said, fumbling at my belt. "And we know what you're up to."

"Do you?" Hugh Richmond said. He was dressed in a blue velvet gown over a long white shirt. Bright yellow stockings kept his feet protected from the Marsden Hall draughts.

"Yes. And I have a knife here," Meg went on, snatching it from my belt. "I am an expert at throwing. Put your weapon down, or this knife will be in your throat, you murderer."

The young man's eyes opened wider. "I haven't got a weapon!" he said quickly.

"Then what's that in your hand?"

"A letter!" he said, holding it up to his candle.

At that moment Grandfather's door clicked, then swung open. He was wrapped in a grey blanket and squinted in the light from the candle. "What is it?" he demanded.

"I've a letter for you. It'll explain why I want to talk to you," Hugh said nervously, looking from the knife to the old man and back to the knife.

"He wants to murder you!" Meg warned.

Grandfather peered down the passageway towards us and sniffed. "He won't be the first."

"The letter will explain," said Hugh.

"I don't have my eyeglass with me," Grandfather complained.

"I'll read it for you," I offered.

"Good idea," Meg whispered, and we moved across to the old man's room.

He opened the door wider. "Your grandmother's asleep next door," he said. "She has the ears of a bat, so keep your voices down."

Hugh Richmond lit another four candles from his own and we sat on the old man's bed in a pool of yellow light. I broke the seal on the letter and unfolded it. "It's Lord Lambton's seal," our visitor said quickly.

I held it up to one of the candles and looked at the picture that was pressed into the wax. It was similar to the Marsden coat of arms. But where we had St George killing a dragon, Lord Lambton had an image of a knight dressed in spiked armour chopping at a giant serpent. It was the old legend of Young John Lambton who had rid our district of the terrible Lambton Worm about two hundred years before.

"It's the Lambton seal," I said.

"So let's see what his lordship has to say to me, shall we?"

The writing was neat and looping and clearly done by his lordship's secretary. "'My dear Clifford,'" I read, "'I hope you are in good health and enjoying a quiet life now you have handed over the estate to your son James.'"

Grandfather had a long fine nose that he used to show more feelings than other people did with their whole body. With sniffs, snorts, flaring and pinching of nostrils, tilting the head to look down or around it, he made his feelings clear. He even had a way of twisting the nose to show that he was deep in thought. This time he gave the long, slow sniff that meant, "I would like to agree with you, but I'm afraid I can't." What he said was, "I think I retired a little too soon. I was saying to William only this afternoon, I feel I have some use left in me."

"Shall I go on, Grandfather?" I asked.

"Yes, my boy," he said graciously and pulled down the tip of his nose till it was as hooked as any falcon's.

"'I am sending this letter to Hugh Richmond, a young man who is cleverer than he looks.'"

"Oh, I say!" Hugh blinked and rose to his feet. "I don't think I was meant to hear this!"

"Sit down," Grandfather snapped.

"Yes," Meg said, with a wave of my dagger. "Sit down."

I read on. "'For as long as anyone can remember there has been trouble on the Borders of Scotland. You were in the thick of it in the days of His Majesty King Henry VIII. Now Her Majesty's Secretary of State, Sir Robert Cecil, has asked me to help with a new danger from the north. Since you know more about the Borders than any Englishman living, I am sending Richmond to you for advice before he sets off on a most dangerous mission. I can say no more in this letter. Destroy it when you have read it. Richmond's task is extremely secret and no one even knows that he is visiting you. His excuse is that he is bringing a message to your son about the trial. Tell no one, or Richmond's life will be in danger. He will explain to you what he wants. With all good wishes, Lambton.'"

We sat in silence for a long time after I had finished reading the letter. Finally Grandfather rose and crossed to a table at the side of his bed. He picked up a large black Bible and brought it towards us. "William, place your right hand on the Bible. You too, Meg." We did as he said. "You should not have read the letter. I see that now. But, since you have, there's only one thing for it."

"I know," I said.

"Swear that you will never repeat anything you have read or heard regarding Hugh Richmond and his mission."

Meg and I swore on the Bible before the old man returned it to the table.

"Now, Master Richmond, what's this all about?"

"Should the boy and girl remain?" he asked.

"They've sworn," the old man said, and tilted his head back to look down his nose. That meant, "Do you dare argue with me?"

Hugh Richmond shrugged and pulled the velvet robe tightly around him. "The new danger from the north," he began. "The raids have started again. Scots are crossing the border, stealing English cattle and sheep and killing anyone who tries to stop them."

"Yes, yes," Grandfather said sourly. "We've suffered Scottish Reivers all my life. But that's nothing new."

Richmond nodded slowly. "The way it has been is this. The Scots steal from the English farmers, so the English organize a raiding party and steal their stock back again. Either that, or they take some other Scottish stock to make up their losses." Hugh Richmond had a way of waving his hands while he was talking that was fascinating to watch. It seemed his right hand was England and his left hand Scotland.

"I know, I know. Why are you telling me this?"

Richmond went on patiently. "It is all so pointless. And it seemed that everyone on the border was seeing sense after all this time. The raids had almost stopped. But now there's something new and more terrifying happening." His eyes were wide as he told his story. We three listeners were now wide-eyed and open-mouthed too.

"What?" I croaked.

"The English raiding parties who have crossed the border have not come back! Not one man! These are the most vicious fighters in England. The best riders, who know the region like you know Marsden Manor. And they are disappearing." Hugh raised a long, fine finger and waved it at Grandfather. "Now, in all your years of fighting on the Borders, have you ever come across anything like that?"

Grandfather scowled. "No," he admitted.

"The Queen does not want to send an army. It would start a war. Her Secretary of State has a system of sending single men that he calls 'spies' into enemy countries. I have been one of his spies for five weeks now. I've been learning about the Spanish problem. I was due to go to Spain to see what effect the death of King Philip of Spain has had on the people. Is the new King planning to send a second Armada against us?"

"Hah! Not if he has any sense!" Grandfather said. "Not after what happened to the last one."

"But the last time we were ready!" Hugh said. "If we

knew about another one, we'd start building more ships, making more cannon, fortifying our ports and harbours now! Not when the Spanish set sail. It will be too late then."

"But why have you been sent to Scotland?" Grandfather said.

"The Spanish work needed someone good at codes and secret messages," the young man sighed. He flapped a hand. "I'm absolutely hopeless at all those numbers and things. But I am absolutely brilliant at disguises. I've got all the voices and I look wonderful in all the costumes! So Sir Robert Cecil sent me to Scotland instead. I've been chosen."

My grandfather covered his eyes with his hands in a brief moment of despair. "What do you know about Scotland?" he asked quietly.

Hugh Richmond spread his hands. "Very little."

"And that's why you've come to me?"

"It is."

"Then I can tell you one thing for a start. You'll have to change those dreadful clothes! You'll stand out like a seagull in a flock of crows. They may be fit for the streets of London and you may not look odd on the streets of Madrid. But on the Borders you'll be talked about ten miles in advance of your journey. Once you get beyond the River Tyne then you're in a wild country where every stranger may be your enemy."

"He can get a riding jack in Newcastle," Meg suggested.

"What's that?"

"It's a quilted leather jacket with steel plates inside to turn away daggers," she explained.

"Sounds quite dreadful," Hugh muttered.

"You'll have to wash off that awful perfume, or the Scots will smell you half an hour before you arrive," Grandfather said. He seemed grimly amused.

"I'll simply stop using it when I bathe," said Hugh.

"Bathe!" Grandfather laughed. "Where on earth do you imagine you are going to bathe? The rivers run down from the Cheviots and they're freezing even at this time of year! The houses don't waste precious water on bathing. Only the great castles between here and Edinburgh will have baths."

"What about the inns where I'll be staying?"

"They use water to brew their ale, not to waste on bathing. Anyway, there are few taverns to stay at once you get into the really wild country. You'll carry a sleeping blanket on your back and a light tent on your pony if you want to look like a borderer. You'll sleep under trees – or under the stars most nights," Grandfather explained.

"It sounds quite ghastly," Hugh sighed.

"God's nails!" Grandfather exploded. "You should be used to it! You're a soldier."

"Who's a soldier?" he asked.

"You are!"

"No, I'm not!"

"You said you were in the service of the Queen."

"As a *spy*."

"But you were a soldier, surely."

"No, I wasn't. I was an actor!"

For once Grandfather was at a loss to know what to say. His nose curled up in a curious display of disgust. "What … what … what on earth use is an actor? The Queen needs soldiers!"

"No!" Hugh said, with a wave of the hand. "Soldiers do the fighting. But she needs people like me to find out other people's secrets."

I nodded. "You can pretend to be someone else. That must be useful."

"Exactly!" Hugh said. "I worked for the Chamberlain's theatre company until the plague closed the theatres. A lot of the actors took to spying to make some money. They do say Mr Shakespeare himself has done some spying."

"You know William Shakespeare?" I said, awed at the thought. I'd heard so much about him and was desperate to go to London to try for a place in his acting company.

"Never mind that now," Grandfather grumbled. "You may be able to mix with people in London or Spain, but you'll never be able to mingle with Border people. You don't know them."

"I do a lovely Scots accent," Hugh said.

Grandfather was turning a dangerous purple-red. "Master Richmond, there is more to disguising yourself as a Scot than putting on some voice. I've seen birds called parrots from South America that can do that." He added spitefully, "And they dress in bright feathers like you, too."

"But that's why I've come to you. Lord Lambton hoped you could tutor me," said Hugh. For the first time he looked a little unhappy.

"I don't have a spare ten years," Grandfather said. "There are men in Northumberland who can pass themselves off as Scots. They've lived on the Borders so long they know the ways of the old enemy. Why didn't Sir Robert Cecil send one of them?"

Hugh clasped his hands together as if he were praying. "Sir Robert did consider them. But he says that they are too close to the Scots. They will raid with the Scots as often as they will fight against them. He doesn't trust the English on the Borders. He says the people who'll lose most in a Scottish war will be people like you. That's why he sent me to Lord Lambton and why Lord Lambton sent me on to you."

Grandfather's back straightened and he looked past the candle-glow into the darkness beyond the window. "He's a clever man, that Cecil. He could be right. The borderers will simply join the Scots if there's war. They'll survive. But manors like Marsden will be torn apart and shared among the winners like the Roman soldiers shared Our Lord's clothes while He was pinned to the cross."

"So you'll help me?" the spy asked.

"I will help you in the only way possible," Grandfather said and he raised his chin. "I will go with you."

And a voice from the darkened doorway said, "No, you will not."

CHAPTER SEVEN

"I have almost forgot the taste of fears"

They say that Marsden Hall has ghosts. For a moment I thought I was looking at one. Grandmother stood there wrapped in a sheet. Her white hair hung down over her shoulders and she looked like an avenging spectre.

I couldn't remember seeing her without her face powdered with heavy white lead. Her skin was yellow and blotched and frail as a moth wing. She stepped forward.

"You are a foolish old man," she said.

Grandfather rose slowly to his feet to face her. "I am," he said. "You've always said so and now you know that you are right."

"You are not fit to ride to Newcastle."

"I am not going to Newcastle, dear heart. I am going over the Borders into Scotland."

"You'll die."

"We'll all die."

"You'll die sooner," Grandmother said, her voice rising angrily.

"But I will die serving my queen, not lying in some cold bed."

"You have served your queen, her sister, her brother and her father before that. Now leave it to the young."

"The young need help."

"Let them help themselves."

"Not while it's in my power to help them."

"You are not only a foolish old man, but a stubborn one too."

"You know that, my sweet, after all the years we've been married."

Grandmother started blinking rapidly, and I realized she was crying. "I will not permit it," she said, her voice breaking.

"The Queen's Secretary of State has asked me to help and this is my best way of helping. It's as if the Queen herself has asked me."

"I'm asking you not to," Grandmother said. She took a step towards her husband. For a few silent seconds their gazes met. It was Grandfather who let his eyes drop first.

"Eleanor," he said softly, "I cannot let this young man go to his death while I sit on my bench in the garden and do nothing. He needs me to look after him."

"And who will look after you?"

I knew then that there was only one answer to that. "I will," I said. "When a knight goes into battle he needs a squire."

Suddenly Meg was standing by my side. "And a squire always has a servant to look after them both."

"It's no place for a girl," I said. I wished I could have bitten my tongue and swallowed it. Meg's face collapsed into an expression of hurt and disappointment. She quickly smoothed it in a show of, "I couldn't care less." But I knew I'd upset her and it would take her a long time to forgive me. What I didn't know was how she would plot her revenge. I wanted to say, "Sorry." My careless tongue refused to shape the word. The moment passed. It's moments like that that can change your life.

Grandmother's eyes showed only defeat. Defeat and love. "The old fool is in good company, then," she said. "I will search the chest for your riding gear and weapons. When will you leave?"

"After James has left for York?" said Grandfather, turning to Hugh Richmond.

"It's best if no one knows that we're going. It's better if Sir James doesn't know you've gone. He may tell someone in York and there are Scottish spies everywhere. England is not the only country to employ people like me," Hugh said.

"Why would my son talk about our venture?" Grandfather asked stiffly.

"Because he may be truly proud of you," Hugh replied.

Grandfather thought about it. "No. No. He'd be ashamed of having such a foolish old man for a father."

Grandmother managed a small smile. "And he'd be right." She turned to Meg, Hugh and me, and said, "If the old blockhead is going to Scotland to die, he'll need his sleep."

Hugh gave a low bow of the kind that actors do on stage and left the room. Meg and I followed. As I closed the door behind me I heard Grandmother say, "So now we know why the crow flew three times round the house and who is going to die."

I don't think I slept much for the rest of the night. Somehow I had talked myself into joining an adventure that could lead to death for all of us. I remembered my grandfather's childhood dream of all those years ago. I was also beginning to wonder how it would feel to be chopped into pieces by a Scottish broadsword.

I got out of bed at first light, but Father was already up

and bullying servants into packing and preparing for his journey to York. "My best black robe, not the one I wear for the local court!" he shouted at an unfortunate manservant. "And I'll take two horses for myself in case one goes lame. I'd better travel with the ostler from the stables, my secretary, a cook and a personal servant – and fetch one of the men from the village as a bodyguard. Make sure you pick a clean one. Oh, and ask the priest if one of his young helpers can travel with me as my chaplain. A man is judged by the number of servants he keeps," he said as he marched through the hall, waving his riding rod. There was a red spot of excitement on each pale cheek.

My mother walked behind him and, without fussing, made sure he had everything he would need. She packed gifts for Lord and Lady Lambton including some fine deep-green cloth woven from the wool of Marsden Manor sheep, a leather-bound prayer book and a silver candlestick with the Marsden crest stamped on it.

"A little expensive," my father grumbled.

"It does no harm to remind Lord Lambton of his most important tenant. When he looks at the candlestick he'll remember us here at Marsden Hall," my mother told him.

Father's chest expanded. "Of course," he said. "I had thought of giving him a pair of candlesticks myself."

"The other one's a little damaged," Mother reminded him. "You dropped it on the floor."

"Should have had it repaired by the silversmith in Wearmouth."

"You said we couldn't afford it, dear."

Father grunted and went to whip the stable boy into action. Meg served breakfast for Hugh Richmond, my grandparents and me. She was quiet that morning.

The Marsden family usually ate dinner in the main hall because we liked to stand by the great fireplace and tell our tales. Most other families ate in one of the private rooms off the main hall; we had breakfast in a small room now. It kept us out of Father's way and allowed us to make our plans. I picked at my eggs with very little appetite. My stomach was as knotted as Meg's wild chestnut hair. I felt her eyes resting on me from time to time, eyes as cold and green as the sea.

Grandfather gave Meg silver to go to Newcastle to buy us the clothes and supplies we needed. She would take a kitchen boy with her to help her drive the small cart. It was ten miles to the north and she'd be away all day. We couldn't hope to set off before tomorrow morning.

"And you, William, can go into the village and find Wat Grey. We'll need ponies for the journey. Buy us five. One each to ride, one to carry our packs and one to take as a spare," Grandfather said.

"I won't need one," Hugh said. "I have the finest chestnut mare north of the Humber."

Grandfather looked at him with some pity. "Master Richmond. We shall be travelling over rough moorland and bogs. We'll be following tracks deep in mud and hills with slippery bare rocks. If your horse gets twenty miles without breaking a leg and I doubt if it would – then it would be stolen as soon as you rode into a village."

"I'd never take my eyes off it," Hugh said.

"Then the Reivers would take your eyes out of your head," the old man told him. "I tried to explain last night; any show of fine clothes or fine animals will attract every thief in Northumberland – and there are more thieves than there are houses, believe me."

Hugh sighed and looked worried.

"What should I look for, Grandfather?" I asked.

"Ask Wat Grey for hobblers or bog trotters he'll know what you mean. They're small, but keep their feet anywhere and go all day without a rest. We want quiet ones – the Reivers just turn them away at the end of the day and the little things are still there the next day, ready for work. No hay or fancy oats for them," Grandfather explained. "Don't worry if they look shaggy and ungroomed. They're meant to. Just check that their feet are sound and take them along to Robyn Smith to have their hooves trimmed and new shoes put on."

"Anything else?" I asked. My grandfather put his lips close to my ear and whispered one last instruction. A few words of persuasion for the horse trader. I grinned and stood up. "I'll be back some time this afternoon," I said.

My mother stopped me and said, "What's going on, William?"

"Ask Grandfather," I said awkwardly.

I hurried through the garden to the path that led to the village. It was a bright enough day, but the wind was chilly coming off the river and there were the first signs of autumn in the trees.

The Black Bull tavern stood near the crossroads, as large and forbidding on the outside as it was dull and filthy inside. The door was open and the smell of stale beer and wine mixed with human sweat made me pinch my nostrils in disgust.

Michael the Taverner lay on the floor, surrounded by overturned tankards. A greasy apron was stretched tight over his enormous belly and his mouth hung open. Apart from the innkeeper's soft snoring, the only sound was the yellow-eyed dog crunching a bone on the floor. I couldn't bring myself to touch the man, or even poke him with my shoe. I shouted, "Michael! Michael Taverner!"

He gave one great snort and raised his head, squinting up at me with red-rimmed eyes. "Whah?" he mumbled.

"I'm looking for Wat Grey."

"What for?"

"No, Wat Grey."

"I mean what do you want him for?" he snarled angrily.

"That's my business."

"Then find him yourself," he said. He sat up, grabbed a table, and hauled himself to his feet.

"He won't thank you for turning business away," I said.

"Business?" a voice said. Then a pinched, fox face peered from behind an overturned table. Perhaps foxes have cleaner faces, though. "Morning, Master Marsden!" the little man said cheerfully. "How is your family? All suffering a slow death from the plague, I hope?"

"I'm afraid not. They're all very well, Master Grey."

"Pity," he sniffed, and wiped his nose on the sleeve of his leather jerkin. He walked to the door and blinked in the morning sunlight as if it hurt. It probably did. His teeth shone yellow and green like old cheese. "You want a horse?"

"No, I want hobblers," I said.

"Ah. Going to Scotland, are you?" he said quickly. He may have been sleepy, but his mind was sharp as the September air.

"No ... just across the Tyne. No further than Morpeth."

"Ahh," he said. I could tell he didn't believe me. "I have some Galloways down by the river meadows. Care to walk down and take your pick?"

The man hurried to walk alongside me down the sloping path through the edge of the wood to the river.

"They're not stolen, I hope."

"I've never stolen a horse in my life!" he cried.

"You've been in the stocks half a dozen times that I know of," I told him.

"Only because your father the magistrate has a nasty suspicious mind. He's never really proved it."

"He'd have hanged you if he had," I said.

Wat Grey shrugged his bony shoulders. "Then he'd have hanged an innocent man. Here are my pretty little ponies. What would you like?"

"I trust you to pick good ones," I said.

The man's short, springing steps hesitated. "You trust me! *You* – trust *me*? Is this your idea of a joke, Master William?"

"No," I replied, walking ahead. "I want five Galloways. I'll pay you twenty-five guineas and I want the best."

"For ten guineas you can take your pick," he offered.

"No. You pick, Wat. If there is one thing wrong with one of the ponies, my grandfather will find you and beat you with the flat of his sword till your teeth drop out."

"What!" he squawked.

"You heard, Wat. These are for my *grandfather*, not *me*. Try to cheat him and he will know."

"You should have said they were for old Sir Clifford," he said. "I'd never rob a great old gentleman like him."

"You would if you thought you could get away with it," I said.

"But I can't," he sighed.

"So you won't."

He knew exactly what he was looking for. The animals were grazing peacefully. They were sturdy, short-legged beasts that stood patiently while Wat threw ropes around the necks of five and led them to me. "Five, eh? The whole

◆ 61 ◆

family going? I could find a nice big stallion for your father. Really big and wild. It would probably break his neck the first time he climbed up on it."

"My father has his own horse," I said.

"Ah, so he's not going with you?" Wat said.

"No."

"So who are the other four for?" he went on.

"Servants."

"Don't worry. These will get you all the way to Edinburgh and back, no trouble."

"I'm not going to Edinburgh, Wat."

"Sorry, I thought you said you were."

I paid him the money. He tested each gold coin with his teeth before he put it into a deep pocket inside his jerkin.

I led the horses towards the smithy. When I turned and looked over my shoulder, Wat Grey was standing at the crossroads talking to a stranger. I could tell from the looks and the nods of the head that he was talking about me. Suddenly the morning air seemed to chill me through. I remembered that Hugh Richmond had said, "There are Scottish spies everywhere." Even Marsden Manor seemed alive with treason.

I waited silently while the smith shod the ponies. It was dinner time before I was back in Marsden Hall.

Grandfather looked at the ponies and nodded his approval. He listened carefully while I told him about Wat Grey's questions and his talk with the stranger at the crossroads. "Don't tell your grandmother. She'll only worry even more."

"She's worried that the journey will kill you," I said. "It's not so much the danger from the Scots."

"Aye, well she has no need to worry. I woke up this

◆ 62 ◆

morning feeling ten years younger now that I have something useful I can do."

"Ten years younger still leaves you twenty years too old!" I said.

His eyes were brighter than I remember. "I have a fine grandson to care for me," he said.

"But I can't fight every Scot in the Borders. Especially if their spies have told them to expect us."

"We'll leave at first light tomorrow," he said. "We'll ride north to Newcastle without going through the village. Perhaps we'll be safe from prying eyes. Perhaps we'll reach there before the spies." He shrugged. "But no one is safe when a queen is dying."

It was dark before Meg returned. She looked tired. There were grey shadows under her sea-green eyes, but her smile was bright enough.

"No problems?" Grandfather asked.

"A lot of people asking questions," she said. "I told them the clothes and weapons were for an actor who's doing a play."

"And that's true in a way," Hugh grinned.

The kitchen boy helped her to unload the cart into the room in the west wing. It was a ground-floor room with a single shuttered window. The door led straight into the stable yard.

Meg brought in the clothing first, placed it on the table and then left the room. The leather jacks with steel plates stitched in were light and comfortable. They fastened at the front with hooks. Hugh and I tried ours on along with the steel bonnets that covered our heads, cheeks and necks. Mine was heavy, but I felt safe inside it.

Grandfather picked up our swords. "William has spent

years practising with a sword. Have you ever fought with one, Master Richmond?" he asked.

"We fight with blunted swords on stage, of course. I died every afternoon in Mr Shakespeare's *Romeo and Juliet*," he said.

Grandfather's nostrils quivered. "Let's hope you don't die on the Borders, Master Richmond. You may find it a little harder to come back to life."

I picked up the wheel-lock pistols that I'd never used. "You can use them to scare birds from our path," Grandfather said sourly. He looked at the neatly rolled blankets and waxed cloth that would make simple tents. "The girl did well. Where is she?"

At that moment the door swung open and a Reiver stepped in. A curious figure. The jack and bonnet and sword were all too large for the small figure that stood there, sword stretched towards my throat, menacing, waiting to slice.

"Good grief!" Hugh exclaimed. "A Scot!"

"Yes, Meg, very frightening," I said. "Now put the sword down before you hurt yourself."

She pushed the steel bonnet up so I could see her face. "These are spare clothes for you. I thought they fitted me quite well." She began to take off the armour and to fold it on the table. "Of course, the Borders are no place for a simple girl," she sighed. "Girls belong in kitchens and the home." She placed the helmet firmly on top of the pile of clothes. "In fact, it would be a good idea to fasten a chain around my ankle and leave me just enough slack to get to the gates of Marsden Hall and no further."

"A chain for your mouth might be more useful," Grandfather muttered.

"I'll ask Robyn the Blacksmith to see if he can make one

to fit, shall I, Sir Clifford?" Meg smiled sweetly.

As Grandfather picked up his sword and tested the flat against his hand, she scurried out of the room. "I think she learns her manners from your grandmother, William," he snorted. He finished dressing in his own old jack and helmet. "I remember the first time I put on the jack and steel bonnet," he said. "It was in the days of Henry VIII."

"Did he ever come back to Marsden Manor?" I asked.

"No," Grandfather said. "He only ever came back to the north once, and even then he stopped at York. But I did get to meet him again. I grew up to take over the care of the manor, and the King sent for all the men in the north to meet him. It was the first time I ever went to London ... and the last time I saw Queen Catherine."

CHAPTER EIGHT

"False face must hide what the false heart doth know"

"I remember that winter well," Grandfather began. "It was one of the coldest winters I've ever known … "

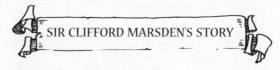
SIR CLIFFORD MARSDEN'S STORY

Henry must have known that it was a hard time to travel. The summons to Hampton Court Palace in London came in mid-winter when the rutted roads were solid with ice. Even with padded doublets, leather gauntlets and woollen cloaks we were all frozen after two miles on the road.

We could barely manage thirty miles a day. My eyes were aching with the cold and my legs too numb to climb down when we reached our night's resting place. But when the King summoned you, then you had to go.

It was more than twenty years since Flodden, of course. With the help of my mother and the steward John Johnston I'd learned to manage my estates. The Marsden lands had never been rich, but in the past few years we'd discovered the black rock they call coal under fields to the north. Workers were hired to dig a pit and bring the coal to the surface. It was taken by wagons down to the River Wear, loaded on to ships and sold in London where we got a fair price.

I wasn't as wealthy as some of my Durham neighbours, but I was able to improve Marsden Hall, add the East Tower and start putting Newcastle glass in some of the windows. I also had the free time and money to train some of the pit men and farm workers into an armed troop to serve the King and defend the manor if the Scots ever came this far south. I was a young man, and the idea of managing farms was too dull. My main pleasure was in the tournaments we fought in the north. I wasn't the greatest horseman, but I never disgraced the Marsden name.

And it was this name as a fighter and leader of a small troop that made me useful to the King. As I rode south with five of my neighbouring captains we tried to guess why he had sent for us. I wondered if there would be a new war with France. We all hoped we wouldn't be sent to crush a rebellion in Ireland.

At last we reached the English fens; a flat place with no shelter from the east winds that swept snowstorms from the sea fifty miles away. Snow drifted deep against the hedges and the black skeletons of trees, while we stumbled and slid off the road towards deep ditches filled with icy water.

By noon we'd had to drag two of our party out of a ditch. They were freezing in the saddle and would die if they had to go another half hour through the fine snow that stung like nettles. When we saw a small castle on a slight rise, we headed towards it without even discussing it.

The house was neglected, its stones crumbling, its overgrown garden pushing through the crusted snow, and wind-beaten shutters slapping noisily against the walls. It was not a place I'd have chosen to stay. It was simply better than the open road and there was a trail of smoke coming from the chimney. I hammered on the door with the hilt of my sword and waited.

"We're travellers from the north," I said to the steward who opened the door a little. "Two of the men need to dry out and warm through. Can you help us?"

"Of course, sir," he said, opening the door wider.

"Thanks," I said. "The King will be grateful."

As I said the words the man stopped. He gave a snarl of pure hatred and began to close the door. I put my boot forward to stop it and he thrust his shoulder against the door. My foot was so frozen that I scarcely felt the pain. I was even angrier than he was and I pushed back. Suddenly he gave way, the door flew open and I tumbled into the hallway. My companions crowded in after me and helped me to my feet.

The steward backed away and stared at us. "Servants of the King are not welcome here," he said hoarsely.

"Where are we?"

"Kimbolton Castle, as if you didn't know." He was breathing fast and his hands were clenched tight. "The King's poisons haven't worked, so now he's sent you to murder her with your daggers, hasn't he?"

We looked at one another, bewildered. "We haven't come from the King. We're on our way to see the King. He summoned us," Lord Birtley explained.

A miserable fire sparked in the fireplace of the hallway. Not a warm welcome, but then it didn't look as if the castle had many visitors. I walked across to the fire and stirred some of the logs. "We mean no harm to anyone," I said. "Just a little warmth, some hot wine and some food. We'll pay."

A door behind the steward opened and a man stepped into the hall. He was small with dark hair, eyes of so deep a brown that they were almost black and a dark olive skin. His neat beard was cut in the Spanish style. His clothes were mostly black. When he spoke his voice had a strong Spanish accent.

"What is going on here? Her Majesty needs quiet," he said. He stood shoulder to shoulder with the steward. "Unless you have come to murder her, of course?"

"We don't even know who lives here. There will be more deaths than one if we don't get our two friends out of their frozen clothes," said Lord Birtley.

The steward and the Spaniard looked at one another. The Spaniard said, "Her Majesty Queen Catherine of Aragon lives here. Since the King cruelly divorced her, she has been a prisoner in this castle. God will free her soon from the miseries of this life, I fear." He turned to the steward and said something in Spanish. The man nodded and told us he would show us to rooms where we could change and eat. He led the way, but I stayed in the hallway. The fire was brighter now and I was warming through. "I'm Clifford Marsden of Durham," I said. "I'm sorry if we don't know what is going on. The happenings in London are a mystery to us."

The man gave a small smile. "I am Doctor Miguel da Sá," he said with a strange stiff bow. We sat at either side of the fireplace and the flames sparkled in his dark eyes as he told me about the Queen's miserable state. "My lady Catherine gave that monstrous king everything. Everything except a son. So he found himself another – woman. I cannot call her a lady. She is known as Anne Boleyn."

"I had heard that, of course," I told him.

"He wanted to divorce my lady Catherine, but she refused. And when the Pope also made problems for the King, he made himself head of his own church. He gave himself a divorce and shut the poor lady away here."

"And she is ill, you say?"

He looked at me with sadness and pain, "Somehow – we don't know exactly how – the evil woman Anne Boleyn managed to place her servants here in Kimbolton. They have poisoned Queen Catherine and all the skills I have cannot help her. It was after she drank a certain Welsh beer, I believe. My lady has seen the new year come. She will not see another."

I looked into the fire and remembered the strong, lively woman who had visited Marsden Manor and had ruled for Henry while the Scots were defeated at Flodden. "I met her once," I said.

The doctor looked interested. "Is that so?"

"I was a child," I said quickly.

He leaned forward eagerly. "My lady Catherine is dying from neglect. The King allows her few visitors. He even refuses to allow their daughter Mary to come here. It would do my lady good to see someone from the past. Will you come and see her?"

I couldn't refuse. Doctor da Sá led the way through to the room he had come from earlier. It was warm in there, but dim, lit only by the fire in the grate. The bed was hung with heavy velvet curtains which were pulled back on the side that faced the fire. The Queen's face was turned towards the flames. If da Sá had not told me it was Catherine of Aragon I would never have recognized her. Her pale cheeks were slack and heavy, her eyes screwed up with pain. Only the plentiful hair reminded me of the Queen I'd met so many years ago.

"You have a visitor, Your Majesty," the doctor said softly.

"Who?"

"Clifford Marsden," I said. "I once served wine for His Majesty when you visited my father at Marsden Manor in the north of England. It was shortly before Flodden."

She looked at me and tried to smile. "Forgive me if I did not recognize you. You have grown up, Clifford," she said.

"A little," I smiled. "I hear the King has changed too."

"He was always cruel," she said. "That has never changed."

"No. Not if he has left you like this."

"I have written him a letter," she said. "I want him to know that I am still his lawful and devoted wife. Mistress Anne Boleyn may have taken my crown, but I will always be his true wife."

"Maybe I could take the letter to him?" I asked. "He's summoned me to Hampton Court."

She nodded and arranged for Doctor da Sá to fetch it. For half an hour I sat by her bed and listened to her talk. She remembered my father and told me how sad she was that he'd died at Flodden. "I was proud of our victory," she said. "But the death of so many good men was bitter as sour wine. Or Welsh beer," she added. She kept returning to Anne Boleyn and the poisoners who'd come to Kimbolton Castle. Finally she stopped talking, and I realized that she'd fallen asleep.

I left her in the care of her doctor and met the others to share a meal. The next morning the wind had swung round to the west and the snow was thawing. As we left, Doctor da Sá handed me the letter for Henry. "May I say goodbye to her?" I asked.

He shook his head. "She is sleeping very heavily. When she is awake she is in pain. It is best to let her sleep."

I rode away from the grim and crumbling castle and hurried down the road towards London.

After the bleak prison of Kimbolton Castle, the King's palace at Hampton Court was a magical world of colour and warmth and noise and richness. We walked past masons and carpenters who were adding another great hall on to the palace.

"It must have cost the King a fortune," I said.

Lord Birtley laughed. "It didn't. The palace was built by Cardinal Wolsey and is the finest palace in England. Of course King Henry was jealous. He threw Wolsey out of power and took his palace."

"The King always gets what he wants," I said.

We slept an exhausted sleep in spite of the carpenters who worked through the night, by the light of candles, to finish the King's new hall. It was not until the next morning that I was allowed to meet the King and deliver the letter. He was sprawled in a huge chair in his apartment, playing cards with a dark-haired woman with a thin face. Her chin was too pointed and her mouth too cruel to be beautiful, but her eyes were large and fine and watched me as I approached the King. It was Anne Boleyn, of course. Her dark hair was so long she could have sat on it. She pushed it back from her face and watched me with cat-clever eyes.

I bowed low and waited for the King to speak.

King Henry was as changed as Catherine of Aragon. His fine body had become bloated and his handsome face almost square. Those eyes that had been too small before were sunk in folds of fat now and edged with red. His whole face was too red, in fact, and the golden beard was darker. The blond hair was thin and his baldness covered with a hat that dripped pearls. "You've a letter, Marsden?" he said. His breath was short. He wouldn't enjoy the day's hunting that he had had in Bournmoor Woods over twenty years before.

"Yes, Your Majesty," I answered, handing it to him.

"Your father still hunting in those fine woods of his?" he asked.

"My father died at Flodden, Your Majesty," I said.

"Did he, by God? I didn't know that! I was in France at the time, of course," he said.

I waited for him to dismiss me, but he said nothing. I stayed kneeling while he tore open the seal and unfolded the package.

His breathing was loud and wheezing. "From that mad-woman Catherine."

"The one who thinks she's still your wife," Anne Boleyn said, smothering a giggle with her hand. I noticed that the hand had six fingers on it. The wise women of Marsden Manor would have said that that was the Devil's sign. They'd have called her a witch and wanted her hanged.

"She says she wants to meet me," the King said quietly.

"No!" the woman said.

"'My dear lord and husband,'" he read, "'The hour of my death draws on quickly ... '"

"But not quickly enough," Anne sneered.

"'You have cast me into many miseries and cast yourself into many cares. I forgive you everything, and I pray God that He will forgive you too. Be a good father to our daughter Mary. Above all, my eyes wish to see you once more.'" He stopped reading, and screwed the letter in his mighty fist. "She has signed it 'Catherine the Queen'."

He threw the ball of paper and it hit my face. I didn't flinch. I heard the door behind me open and a messenger hurried up to the throne and whispered in the King's ear.

The King gave a roar and turned to clutch the woman by the arms and raise her to her feet. "Catherine is dead! She died yesterday afternoon!"

"God be praised!" Anne cried. "Now I am indeed Queen!"

"We must have a feast to celebrate!" he laughed, and limped past where I still knelt on the floor.

I was kneeling there five minutes later when a young woman came and asked me what I was doing. I seemed to have lost the power of speech. "I always thought that we should mourn for the dead and not celebrate," I finally said.

"It depends who has died," the young woman said. She was younger than I, dressed more simply than the Queen, but much prettier.

"Are you a servant here?" I asked.

"I'm a lady-in-waiting to the Queen," she said. "Do I look like a serving maid?"

"Sorry," I blushed. "I don't know much about court life."

"No," she laughed. "And you don't know much about women either, do you?"

"No," I admitted.

"My name is Eleanor," she said, as she led me out of the King's apartments.

"I am Clifford Marsden from County Durham."

She showed me the way back to my apartments where I broke the news of the Queen's death to my travelling companions. That night we went to the chapel and prayed for the soul of the dead Catherine.

Two days later the King had his court ball. He and Anne

dressed in bright yellow costumes – that is the colour they wear in Spain when there is a death in the house. But on King Henry and Anne Boleyn it looked more as if they were dressed to rejoice.

The King danced in the centre of the floor while his courtiers cheered him and told him what a wonderful man he was. There was jousting, but the King had to sit and watch. It seemed his leg wound was hurting too much for him to ride.

The lady-in-waiting, Eleanor, shared our table. She explained that the King's injury had saved someone a beating. "His favourite trick is to appear in disguise," she said. "He enters the tournament as a mystery knight and challenges anyone to battle."

"He could be killed," I said.

Eleanor laughed. "No, he couldn't. Everyone knows it's the King. How could he hide that body? It's like a blown-up pig's bladder that boys play football with. Anyway, they know he has this silly game of appearing in disguise."

I remembered that he'd pretended to be someone else when he came to Marsden Manor. "So the other knights let him win?" I asked.

"Of course," Eleanor said. "The trouble is that that doesn't stop the King from battering them half to death just to show off his strength. He's nothing better than a child in a man's body," she added. Words like that could have led her to dangle by the neck from the end of a rope. King Henry VIII was fond of hanging people.

The King couldn't fight that evening, but he showed his skill at playing the lute and sang a song to Anne Boleyn. It seemed as if he were dancing on dead Catherine's grave and enjoying it.

I was not in the mood to dance, but the young Eleanor led me on to the dance floor. She helped me forget the misery of the poor dead queen of Flodden.

And of course, in time, I married that young woman – but that's another story.

We had our meeting with the King the next day and returned home the day after that.

That was January 1536.

Three weeks later the King took part in a tournament and was knocked from his horse. The old leg wound opened up and never healed for the rest of his life. He was crippled; scarcely able to ride and in pain when he tried to dance.

He was cruel before. Now he began to suffer terrible rages. And when King Henry raged, people died.

Within the year there was a second dead queen. For in May the King had Anne Boleyn's head sliced from her body by a French swordsman. As she knelt and waited for the blow, she prayed, "God save the King and send him long to reign over you. There was never a more merciful king, and to me he was always a good and gentle lord."

CHAPTER NINE

"At least we'll die with harness on our backs"

My grandfather sighed. "The good and merciful Henry was playing his favourite sport of tennis while his second wife was executed. When they brought him news of her successful execution he took a barge across the Thames to meet his new love and next wife, Jane Seymour."

"Poor women," Hugh Richmond said with a shudder. "Do you believe he had Catherine poisoned?"

My grandfather spread his hands and said, "It's possible. The candle-maker at Kimbolton Castle cut open Catherine of Aragon's body to examine it and find out why she had died."

"Why the candle-maker?" Meg asked.

"In the castles of the great lords the candle-maker always has the duty of examining the dead," Hugh explained.

The girl just shook her head, puzzled.

Our guest the spy asked, "What did he find?"

"Henry never allowed the report to be published. But on our way back from London, we stopped off at Kimbolton and found that her coffin was being taken to Peterborough for burial. Her Spanish doctor said he'd watched the candle-maker's examination. He said that Catherine's heart had turned black and no amount of washing would remove the darkness. He felt sure it was poison."

"But what do *you* think?" Hugh persisted.

"I think that Anne Boleyn was wicked enough to arrange it and clever enough to get away with it. Henry hated poisoners, and I doubt if he'd have ordered her death that way. He once heard about a cook who poisoned two guests at a dinner. He said that the best death for such a poisoner would be to be boiled alive in a cooking pot. His lawyers said there was no law that allowed execution by boiling alive. So Henry had a law passed, and that's how the cook was executed."

"Horrible," said Hugh.

"But even if King Henry didn't have Catherine poisoned, he killed her just as surely," Grandfather sighed. "He killed her with hatred, he killed her with insults and he left her to die neglected in that half-ruined castle."

"But, Grandfather," I said, "you haven't told us why the King had sent for you."

"That's true," he remembered. "The King wanted the Durham lords to stir up trouble on the Scottish Borders. He wanted to make sure that the Scots had so much trouble on the Borders that they would never invade again the way they had at Flodden. He wanted trusted men going over into Scotland. We would appear to be cattle-thieving Reivers. In truth we'd be seeing what was going on around the Scottish Lowlands. Seeing if there was any sign of a new invasion by James V."

"You were spies!" Hugh Richmond laughed. "Before Elizabeth and her Secretary of State thought of the idea! You were spying for King Henry VIII!"

"I suppose we were," Grandfather said. "But we were soldiers first."

"I still don't see why he wanted men from Durham," I said. "He already had English Reivers in Northumberland doing all the raiding he wanted, didn't he?"

"But King Henry never trusted them. Even at Flodden he was getting complaints that the Reivers fighting for the English did more damage than the Scots!"

"How could they do that?" Meg asked.

"The Bishop of Durham said that the English Reivers only joined the battle to see what they could steal. When a man fell, they took his horse and armour whether he was an Englishman or Scot. They didn't care. They stole from the army supplies and carried food and horses back to their homes in the Northumberland dales. They even found wounded English on the battlefield and delivered them to the Scots to ransom. Then they shared the money. Is it any wonder King Henry distrusted them?"

It sounded like a dangerous world beyond the Tyne. It was a comfort to have Grandfather with us. I only wished that he'd been fifty years younger.

We were all tired after the late meeting the previous night and the preparations of the day. We planned to be away before first light the next day, so no one argued when Grandfather suggested we should go to bed soon after supper that night.

The next morning was no warmer, but at least the roads were dry and free of mud. Our little army of an old man, an actor and a boy sat astride small horses at the gates of Marsden Manor. There were no crows flying around the tower yet, but I heard their harsh cries as they stirred in the gloomy tree tops of Bournmoor Woods. I wondered how many of us would return.

Grandmother handed Grandfather a silk handkerchief. "Tie it round your neck," she said. "A knight going into battle always wears a gift from his lady."

"We'll be back before October," Grandfather said. "If all goes well."

"Aye. Perhaps."

My mother stood stiff and unhappy. "Take care of him, William," she said.

Grandfather looked at her from under his thick eyebrows, but said nothing. He turned his pony towards the north and nudged it gently with his knees. It began to amble forward. The other ponies followed. The road north ran straight for almost a mile before it turned to join the main road from London to Newcastle. By the time we reached the crossroads the sun had risen blood red and lit the top of Marsden Hall. The ancient limestone shone golden. The tiny figures of the women were still watching as we turned on to the main road.

If I had been honest I'd have admitted I was disappointed. I had hoped Meg would have risen early to say goodbye. It seemed she had not forgiven me. I saw my mother and grandmother raise their hands in farewell.

As I looked back I thought I saw the shadow of a man moving through the woods at the side of the road as if someone were trying to track us without being seen. "Are we being followed?" I said to Hugh Richmond.

"The trick is to pretend you haven't noticed. In time they will show themselves," he said.

Now that he was dressed in riding clothes and away from the hall I could see what Lord Lambton meant when he had written, "'Hugh Richmond, a young man who is cleverer than he looks.'"

We reached the banks of the Tyne by mid-morning and looked across the river to Newcastle. The square, solid tower of the castle had been "new" in the days of the Normans, but now it was stained and weathered. The sandstone had been turned a gritty grey from the foul shroud of smoky air that hung over the town. The river was so crowded with ships that I wondered they didn't collide. Men rowed small coal barges out to the larger ships that waited in the deepest part of mid-river and loaded their cargo into the holds. It looked like back-breaking work.

Grandfather looked over his shoulder and spoke to us. "You remember I told you that I came home after Catherine of Aragon had died? Well, the King began closing the monasteries soon after that. He collected the rents from the monastery lands and when he needed more money he sold the land off. Newcastle here came out of it best. The monks wouldn't allow much coal-mining. Once their lands were sold the miners moved in. Newcastle's built on coal. And it's close to the river here to ship the coal off to London. The Durham mines have much more trouble moving the coal. That's why we're not as rich as King Henry!"

We crossed the Tyne bridge and entered the town where the road north ran between wooden houses that looked so tall they might topple on to us. The noise and smell were sickening. Beggars pulled at our legs as we rode past. Some of the fitter ones tried tugging at our saddle packs. We drew our daggers to chop at hands that got too close. "Of course, the poor used to go to the monasteries for help. When Henry closed them he left these people to beg," Grandfather explained.

The smell of the sooty air was mixed with rotting fish on

the quayside, horse-droppings in the roadway, and human filth from the houses where children ran naked across the street, dodging the churning cartwheels. Drunken sailors roared songs from the quayside taverns, traders shouted and argued at their market stalls, the road was blocked by geese and cows and sheep being driven along them. "Is London like this?" I asked Hugh Richmond.

"London is bigger, of course," he said. "But this is a more frightening place. I think maybe Hell is like this."

We picked our way through the crowds and climbed the steep road from the riverside towards the better houses of the rich that stood in the fresher air. We passed through the West Gate and rode alongside a huge and ruined wall, wide enough for two horses to walk side by side. "That's Hadrian's Roman Wall," Grandfather said. "They say Queen Elizabeth is looking at a plan to repair and fortify it again. The idea is to have forts every mile. If the Scots try to invade they would never be able to capture eighty forts."

"I'd feel safe behind that," Hugh said.

As the road climbed, the houses became fewer and the road lonelier. At last we reached the top of a small hill. Empty moorland stretched ahead of us. In the distance was a sight that made even the mighty wall look as small as a cart rut in the road. A rolling mass of bleak purple hills stood like a barrier ahead of us. I could see no houses, no roads and no easy way through them.

"They must be the Cheviot Hills," Hugh said.

"Yes. That's where the Reivers are at home. They know all the paths and passes and secret places," Grandfather said.

"It looks a dangerous place," the actor said. "Will we be safe sleeping up there?"

"Don't worry," the old man told him. "We'll stay on the plain that runs up the east coast. If we can get to Morpeth by nightfall then we should find a comfortable tavern to spend the night in. It'll be a couple of days before we turn west into the hills."

From the high ground I was able to look back on the grey town. I could see no one trying to follow us secretly. A horseman was coming up from Newcastle at a fast amble. He passed us without a word of greeting. His head was down and his face hidden by a wide-brimmed hat.

"Is this the only road north?" I asked.

"No," Grandfather said. "Why?"

The truth was I was wondering when our secret watcher would pass us. He would have to at some time. He needed to get ahead of us to warn his friends ahead that we were on the way.

"I thought there might be a quicker way," I said.

"No. This is the most direct. The others involve going to the coast at Tynemouth, or up the Tyne valley. We're going the shortest way because I don't want you to get too tired."

"Us!" Hugh cried. "What about you?"

Grandfather kicked his pony on to a fast walk. "I'll be all right. I've ridden this road many times before."

"When you were younger," said Hugh.

"And what about the Earl of Surrey?" the old man said suddenly. "When Surrey led the English army up this road to Flodden he was crippled with rheumatism. He sometimes had to be carried on a stretcher. He was seventy years old, he never complained and he went on to beat the Scots."

"Is that what you want, Grandfather?" I asked.

"One more great deed before I die," he said. "That's all I ask."

He had chosen the strongest pony and we were struggling so hard to keep up with him that we hadn't much time for talk that afternoon. If Grandfather felt the strain of the long ride then he refused to show it. I know it exhausted me. I have never been so pleased to see a town as I was to see Morpeth at the end of the day.

A quieter, cleaner, smaller town than Newcastle, where people knew one another well. As we walked down the main street I could feel a hundred pairs of eyes watching us and a hundred minds wondering what business we had in that place.

The tavern was quiet and clean compared to the Black Bull in Marsden village, but the landlord with the bald and sweating head looked at us suspiciously. He served us mutton stew in silence and had a serving girl show us into a small cold room at the end of long and twisting corridors. Grandfather and I shared one pallet bed with a straw-stuffed mattress while Hugh had the other.

For all my tiredness I lay awake a long time, listening to the scuttering and squeaking sounds as some creatures ran over the ceiling above us. I wondered what had happened to the men who had disappeared when they crossed the border.

Now I'd seen those grim purple hills I began to understand how a king's army could be swallowed up. What chance did three people have? Three people as weak as the scuttering mice. And maybe we were mice walking into some carefully laid trap.

CHAPTER TEN

"And fixed his head upon our battlements"

The next morning we dressed in our Reiver clothes and armour. "Thank goodness my friends in London can't see me now," Hugh groaned.

"Go back to your silk doublet," Grandfather suggested as he lay on his bed. "You'll make a brighter target for the Scottish archers."

"It wouldn't protect me," Hugh sighed, as if he had thought about it seriously.

"We could always ask them to attack us with silk swords," the old man cried, and the actor blushed. "That would only be fair, wouldn't it?"

"I was hoping we wouldn't be attacked at all!" said Hugh.

"He was hoping no one would attack us at all!" Grandfather exclaimed, his voice rising. "The people of Marsden have spent a hundred years hoping the Scots won't attack us. But we don't sit down on our velvet-covered backsides and *pray* that it won't happen. We get up and we do something about it." He shook his head angrily. "At least that's what we *would* do if we *could* get off our backsides!" he ended with a roar.

I suddenly understood. "You can't get up? Is that it, Grandfather?"

"No, I can't!" he hissed. "My mind tells my body to move and my body is refusing."

"Can we help?" Hugh asked.

"Can he help, he asks! Can he help? Yes, he can. He can take my arm and pull me to my feet!"

Hugh and I took an arm each and gently eased the old man up. He was shaking a little and breathing noisily with his mouth open. "Don't just stand there looking at me!" he snapped. "I'm just a little stiff. I'll be all right once I'm back in the saddle."

We dressed quickly and helped my grandfather on with his clothes. As I laced up the jack it seemed to give him new strength and determination. "Now, let's get to breakfast, shall we? See if that miserable landlord has learned how to smile, eh?"

"Perhaps you could teach him," Hugh suggested mildly.

"Perhaps I could," Grandfather answered as he climbed slowly down the stairs. "I know how to smile. It's just so difficult when you're travelling with an ignorant young peacock."

"That's not a kind thing to say about your grandson," the actor said.

"I was talking about *you* – as you know fine well," Grandfather said, trying to glare at Hugh.

The young man put on such an expression of shock and dismay that Grandfather's mouth clamped tight and thin to stop himself from smiling.

I thought that even the gloomy landlord couldn't spoil our spirits that morning. I was wrong. Now he was a picture of sheer misery as he served us bread, cheese and ale. He stood at the table, twisted his broad red hands and looked at the floor. "What's the matter, man?" Grandfather asked.

"I'm sorry, sir, but there has been a misfortune during the night."

"What sort of misfortune?" Grandfather asked.

"It's your ponies, sir."

"They're in your stable."

"They are – at least four of them are. Unfortunately one of them seems to have disappeared."

Grandfather slapped both hands flat on the table. If he hadn't been so stiff he'd have pushed himself to his feet. "What do you mean, disappeared? Disappeared through witchcraft?"

"No, sir."

"Disappeared through some heavenly miracle?"

"No, sir."

"Disappeared behind Merlin's cloak of invisiblity?"

"No, sir. It's been taken away."

Grandfather spoke slowly and uttered each word clearly. "If you mean it has been stolen, then why can you not say so?"

The landlord swallowed hard. "Stolen, sir. Stolen. I've been landlord here for twelve years this Christmas and I've never had a horse stolen from my stable. Never."

"So what went wrong this time?" I asked.

"Oh, sir," the man said, turning towards me and away from the fire of Grandfather's gaze. "It was a boy. He said he was with Sir Clifford Marsden of Marsden Manor. He described all three of you and said the young gentleman, Master William, needed one of the ponies to ride over to the castle. The groom in the stables saddled up a pony and handed it over. It was only when the boy rode off down the main street that he suspected it was a trick. He asked if you were looking for your horse. I told him you'd gone to bed."

Grandfather rubbed his eyes tiredly. "So you're going to pay me for a new pony?"

"I haven't got the money, sir," the miserable man said.

"Then what do you plan to do?"

"I could give you my donkey," he offered.

"I don't need a donkey," Grandfather said. Then he added, "I am already travelling with two donkeys," and he looked at Hugh and me. "I want the remaining spare pony loaded with supplies for ten days."

"Yes, sir."

"I want no charge for last night's stay."

"Of course not, sir."

"And I want a free night at this inn when we return from Hexham in two weeks' time."

The man looked grateful. "Of course, sir."

I knew that Hexham was to the south-west while we were heading to Alnwick in the north. I understood what Grandfather was doing and didn't argue.

"So what did this boy look like?" I asked.

"The groom said he was small, but he had a wide-brimmed hat so he couldn't see his face."

"His clothes?"

"Dark riding clothes, but no riding boots, only shoes. The clothes were dusty as if he'd come a long way."

Grandfather waved a hand and said, "Leave us, land-lord." The man gave a bow as if we were royalty and almost backed out of the room.

"A thief?" Hugh said, but he didn't sound too sure.

"Either that, or an enemy trying to weaken us," I said, thinking of the figure who'd followed us. He could have been a boy who had been watching and following from Marsden Manor. The man who'd ridden past us was too tall and old to be the thief and anyway, he'd been wearing boots.

"Why didn't he take all our ponies?" Hugh asked.

"Maybe he plans to take them one at a time. It could be that he is working alone."

Grandfather shook his head and rose stiffly, but without our help. "You two have sharper eyes than me. I expect you to keep your eyes open for anyone suspicious – anyone on the road ahead, the road behind, or the paths to the side."

All that day we rode. My neck was sore with constantly twisting to look round. There were maybe three times when, as we reached the brow of a hill and I could look back a long way, I thought I spotted someone on a pony. It could have been an innocent traveller. But when we stopped, he stopped.

By late afternoon we were in Alnwick and ready for another overnight stay. We rode through the small gateway in the town walls. The huge castle looked down on us. The people in the streets seemed even more unfriendly than those in Morpeth. It could have been our Reiver clothes, or it could be that they were so much nearer the border and more afraid of armed riders.

Grandfather explained this as we rode through the market where traders were loading their unsold animals and food on to carts. Beggars whinged and asked for some of the leavings. Sometimes they were rewarded with a turnip. More often they were rewarded with a boot. "This place is a nest of treachery. King Henry VIII gave the Earl of Northumberland the task of clearing the Reivers from the east of the Borders. And who was the biggest thief and murderer? Why, the Constable of Alnwick Castle himself William Lisle. This William Lisle had been arrested once and he was set free from prison in Newcastle by the Scots and the English Reivers working together. He fled to safety in Scotland. That's how much the border mattered to some of these villains."

"What happened to William Lisle?" I asked.

"King Henry decided that if the Scottish and English Reivers could work together, then so could the Scottish and English governments. They chased him so hard that William Lisle had no peace on either side of the border."

"Did they catch him?" Hugh asked.

"Not exactly. The old Earl of Northumberland's father had been a close friend of William Lisle. Of course, William was sure that the young Earl would be just as friendly." My grandfather stopped his horse and looked down the long cobbled street that led to the dismal castle on a slight hill. "William Lisle took a great gamble. With fourteen of his leading captains he walked along this street they call Canongate. The young Earl of Northumberland was riding back from church towards the castle there. The two men met about here. Lisle and his men were wearing only plain white shirts – even though it was January. They wore just one other thing. A rope around their necks."

"They were looking for forgiveness," said Hugh.

"Even my grandson could work that out," Grandfather snapped, impatient at being interrupted.

"Sorry, sir."

"As I was saying, they gave themselves up and looked for mercy. Now, young William, what would you have done if you had been the Earl?"

"I'd have forgiven him. Especially if he was a friend of my father."

Grandfather turned to Hugh. "And you, Master Richmond?"

"Oh, forgiven him. After all, he was on the same side."

Grandfather nodded, satisfied. "Exactly!" he said.

"Which just goes to show why you need someone like me to help you." He kicked his pony forward into a gentle walk. "These are the Borders, where the King's law had been ignored for years. King Henry wanted to show these Reivers, Scots and English, that he was strong. And what did the King do when he wanted to show his strength? He killed people."

"He executed William Lisle?" I said. I was shocked that a man who had surrendered peacefully should be treated so harshly. "It doesn't seem fair."

"Exactly, my boy. In the Borders you have to forget about fair and unfair. Lisle was hanged and his body cut into quarters. They hanged one of the quarters up above the gateway of the castle here, just to teach the Reivers a lesson. Don't expect any mercy."

We passed under the dark gateway where a guard asked what our business was. "Is Sir John Forster still Captain of the Guard?" Grandfather asked.

"He is," the guard said.

"Then tell him Sir Clifford Marsden is here to visit him. He won't believe it, but tell him to remember Pinkie."

"Your brain is cracked, old man," the guard sneered.

"Not as cracked as yours will be if my friend Hugh Richmond here hits you with his sword. He is the greatest fighter in London, and he enjoys cutting traitors into quarters and hanging bits of them above castle gateposts. Before he kills you, can you tell me which bit of you you'd like to hang over Alnwick Castle?"

The man's unshaven jaw dropped and he snivelled, "There's no need to be like that," before running off to fetch his captain.

Hugh blew a long breath through his cheeks. "You're a better actor than me!" he said.

Grandfather nodded. "The Borders, my boy. The Borders. You make up your own rules here. There's no point in fighting fair if your enemy is going to cheat."

The guard came running back and asked us to follow him to the Captain's apartments. I turned and looked over my shoulder. The street was emptying as the farmers hurried home before the purple darkness from the hills swallowed them. "If a boy on a pony tries to follow us in here, don't let him in. If you do, Hugh Richmond will have your head looking down from the guard tower."

The man was so frightened now that his face was quivering as he nodded. I was learning the ways of the Borders.

We climbed the stone steps up to the Captain of the Guard's apartment. We moved slowly since Grandfather was very stiff and tired. The evening was turning dark and chill, but the main room was lit by a blazing fire. A man stood with his back to the flames. He was not tall, and his iron-grey hair was cropped short. He was at least as old as my grandfather, but he looked fitter and his eyes were sharper.

His face showed no expression as he glanced at me, then at Hugh Richmond. Finally he looked at Grandfather and one dark-grey eyebrow lifted. "Clifford Marsden, you old rogue. So the story is true."

"John Forster, you old villain!" Grandfather said, scowling. He took two steps towards the Captain of Alnwick Castle Guard and wrapped his arms around him. "I never thought we'd meet again this side of the gates of Hell. Why aren't you down there in Hell with the Devil now?"

Forster put welcoming arms round my grandfather and slapped his back. "I'm too wicked even for the Devil to take me. So I just live on. The same as you."

Grandfather released his old friend and placed a hand on

each of his shoulders. "So what story have you heard?" he asked seriously.

"The story that you were headed north again with your grandson and a stranger in fancy London clothes."

My grandfather sank back into an oak armchair by the fire and looked angrily into the flames. "Someone saw us in Morpeth and rode ahead?" he asked.

John Forster shook his head. "I have a feeling that the story came from your own Marsden estate. I think news went around that you were buying horses and jacks and weapons. It's difficult to keep secrets in this area. Secrets are usually worth money to someone."

"So this spy rode ahead and warned people that we were on our way?"

"He did," the old Captain agreed. "One of my men heard the story in the tavern this afternoon."

"I don't understand," I said. "This afternoon I looked back on the road and I'd have sworn we were being followed. A spy can't have been ahead of us and behind us at the same time."

"No," Hugh said, "but a pair of spies could."

Sir John strode to the door and called for a guard. He gave him hurried instructions, then came back to the fireside. "You are safe enough here," he promised. "I'll have beds prepared and you can eat with me in about half an hour."

"Thank you," Grandfather said warmly. He turned and looked at Hugh and me. "People of the Borders have long memories. They never forget an enemy and they never forget a friend."

"And we still have enemies up here," Sir John explained. "So what are you doing risking your life in Alnwick when you could be enjoying a peaceful life in Marsden Manor?"

Grandfather's mouth turned down. "A peaceful death more like. I was bored, John, waiting to die. When the chance came to help Hugh Richmond here, I took it."

"Help him do what?" Sir John asked.

Before Grandfather could answer, Hugh cut in, "I'm sorry, Sir John, but that is a secret."

The two old men looked at one another. Then they looked back at the young man. "Sir John is the Crown's most loyal servant," Grandfather explained. "Not only is he loyal to Queen Elizabeth, but he was loyal to her brother Edward and her father King Henry VIII before that."

"And I am loyal to Sir Clifford," the Captain said. "He saved my life and I owe him for that. I would never betray him or put his life at risk. Never, Master Hugh. Not even under the pain of torture."

Hugh looked embarrassed and muttered, "Sorry ... sorry. I didn't mean to suggest you were a traitor."

Sir John raised a hand. "I'm not offended. If I had been you'd have been testing your sword skills in a duel, young man." He turned to my grandfather and asked, "Haven't you told them the story of the old days on the Borders?"

"Not yet," Grandfather said.

"Perhaps you should. Then Master Richmond can decide if his secret is safe with me."

Grandfather pulled off his cloak, unbuckled his sword belt and laid it on the table. When he was comfortable, he signalled for Hugh and me to sit on the bench at the table and listen.

CHAPTER ELEVEN

"𝕭𝖑𝖔𝖔𝖉 𝖜𝖎𝖑𝖑 𝖍𝖆𝖛𝖊 𝖇𝖑𝖔𝖔𝖉"

SIR CLIFFORD MARSDEN'S STORY

I remember the first time I met John Forster. It was soon after I'd returned from meeting King Henry and Anne Boleyn in London. He was the most dangerous man in England. The King had given him the task of keeping the law on this side of the border. His official title was Warden of the East March. The Scots cattle thieves, the Reivers, were so afraid of his power that they took to raiding the Middle March and the West March. They even started robbing from their own side of the border. Anything rather than face John Forster's East March troopers.

Now King Henry had sent John Forster to Berwick Castle to keep the peace. He then decided that he didn't want peace in the Borders. He sent me and the Marsden men to stir up trouble.

John Forster was a handsome, dark-haired man with dark eyes and a strong chin. Even in the days when long hair was the fashion he kept his short. I met him on the walls of Berwick Castle looking across the border to where Scottish farmers were holding a market. I'd never seen so many Scots in my life. "Do you feel safe with so many of them just outside your walls?" I asked.

John Forster smiled. "They keep Berwick Castle supplied with all the food we need. We'd probably starve without them."

"They're the enemy! They could poison the food!"

"If they did that it would be bad for business. Kill off your best customers and you'll starve."

I was shocked. I'd grown up learning to hate the Scots, and here was the King's warden trading with them. "How do you know the beef you buy hasn't been stolen from English farmers?" I asked.

"If I buy it from English traders, the beef could still have been stolen from English farmers. These Reivers work on both sides of the border, you know. Of course, the English like stealing from the Scots and the Scots like stealing from the English. But both sides will steal from their own people if they have to," he explained.

"It's your job to stop the thieving on this side of the border, though," I said.

He looked at me with some disgust. "You are a stranger to this area, Marsden. The Borders are not like Hadrian's Wall down on Tyneside. They are just a wild wasteland with mountains and valleys. There are more tracks across that desert and more secret, sheltered spots than there are people in Berwick. The Scots have a valley up near Edinburgh that they call the Devil's Beef Tub. And it's called that because it's full of English cattle that they've stolen."

"Does the King know that?" I asked.

Forster glared at me as if I were threatening him. "Give me a thousand men and I'll stop most of the thieving. But what does the King send me? You and twenty of your Durham farmers. Ha!"

"We aren't here to help you stop the raids. We are here on a much more serious mission," I said quietly. Secretly I wondered if I should be trusting him.

"What's that?" he asked sharply.

I took a deep breath of the cool air that was whipping over the grey-green waves of the North Sea to the east. "I am here to attack the Scots."

He blinked and looked as if he wanted to step back from this Durham madman that the King had sent.

"With twenty men?"

"Not exactly. We will be joined by your own men and by some of the leading families in the north. We won't be going to war with Scotland. We'll be stealing and ruining the farms on their side of the Borders," I said.

"You are mad!" he cried. "I've spent two years bringing peace to the area! Why would I want trouble?"

"Because your king has ordered it," I said. "He hates the Scots. He doesn't want to give them this peace you've brought. He wants their forces so busy dealing with cattle raids that they don't have the chance to invade England."

"So he's sent you to steal Scottish cattle?" he asked.

"Yes."

"Have you ever stolen a cow?"

"No."

"A sheep?"

"No."

"Have you ever burned a house, or attacked a castle?"

"No."

He nodded. "The Scots won't sit back and let you take their cattle."

"I know."

"They will fight. And in the fight they will probably capture you. They will hold you to ransom. If your family don't pay, then they'll hand you over to their warden who will probably hang you. I don't suppose you've ever been hanged either, have you, Marsden?"

I didn't answer that. "It's the King's orders," I said.

John Forster leaned on the castle battlements and looked over to the bleak, dark hills to the west. "They do say that the King is sick in his mind. I didn't believe them until now."

"So you won't help?" I asked.

He looked at me and grinned suddenly. "I'll tell you a secret, Marsden. There are six wardens on the Borders – three on either side. The others spend as much time helping their thieving friends as they spend punishing their thieving enemies. I've always thought it must be a more exciting way to spend the time up here at the end of the world. I'll help."

And so I'd crossed my first hurdle. John Forster didn't like me very much, but at least he was going to help me. He explained life on the Borders and the way the Reivers worked. I had no idea the place was so violent. "These people live on poor land," he explained. "They can build a house in a day. It doesn't matter to them if it's burned down. They just build another! Of course these houses are made of mud or turf and they're not comfortable, but it's a sort of life."

"I saw stone towers as we rode through Northumberland," I said.

"They're Pele Towers. The richer families have them and the villagers can bring cattle into the shelter of the walls when there's a raid."

"Isn't it too late by then?" I asked.

"Not always. There are beacons on top of every tower. When a troop of Reivers appear, they light the beacon fire and warn everyone to take cover. If they light four beacon fires, then we know it's a small army on the way."

"And do the Scots do the same when the English attack them?"

"Of course. And that's why the Reivers prefer to attack at night. They can surprise the farmers and drive the cattle off before anyone knows they're there. Of course it's difficult reiving in the dark, but some of the old Reivers know every path for a hundred miles blindfolded. Most like a little moonlight, though."

From the heights of the battlements of Berwick Castle I heard a rumbling noise. People were shouting. John Forster leaned forward and stretched out an arm to point to the massive gatehouse of the castle. A man rode through on a piebald pony followed by a woman on a blue roan. He was carrying a weapon that all the armed men in Northumberland seemed to carry – a lance about twice the length of a man. But on the steel tip of this lance there was a piece of dark turf. And the turf was on fire.

"A hot trod!" Forster cried. I had no idea what he meant. I watched as the piebald pony clattered on to the cobbles of the courtyard and the rider jumped down. Soldiers and castle servants gathered around him curiously and from the babble of noise I heard John Forster's name cried.

"Here, man!" the Warden called and the crowd looked up.

"A hot trod!" the crowd were crying, and the soldiers were running to their quarters and coming out with weapons and tugging on armoured jacks.

John Forster was moving quickly to the stone stairs that led down to the courtyard while I tried to keep up with him. "Arm your men, Marsden," he called over his shoulder. "They can have their first lesson in reiving now."

I found one of the Marsden men and quickly ordered

him to gather our troop and fetch my own weapons and horse. Then I pushed my way through the crowd to where the Warden was talking to the woman.

"They took everything," she raged. "Ten cattle and fifteen sheep. How am I supposed to get through the winter?"

"Let's catch them first and get your cattle back," John Forster was saying, trying to soothe her. "Which way did they go?"

"And they pulled my house down! Tied a rope to a door post and pulled till it fell down! Why did they have to do a thing like that?"

"Did you see which way they went?" the Warden was saying patiently.

"If my husband had been there, he'd have taken his sword to them. But I'm no good with a sword."

"If your husband had been there and had taken a sword, then they would probably have beaten him till he was flat as his own blade."

The woman glared as if Forster were to blame. "I hope you hang them when you catch them," she spat.

"But I won't catch them unless you tell me who took the animals and which way they headed."

"Didn't I tell you? It was that Scottish hog with the red beard and no nose!"

"Nebless Clem," Forster nodded.

"And they headed over Thrust Pick towards Murders Rack," she said, pointing to the gloomy hills.

Forster nodded briskly and turned to me. "This time I'll ride out with you."

"Don't you usually?" I asked.

Forster's eyes narrowed and he leaned forward till he was breathing in my face. "There are gangs of men who would like nothing better than to see me dead," he explained. "They don't steal English cattle to eat. They steal English cattle so the English warden will go after them. And, when it's getting dark, and we get to a quiet gully, then they turn and attack us. It's my blood some of these gangs want. The Scot who carries my head on the end of a lance will be a hero in his country." Suddenly the Warden grinned. "Such a shame to do that to such a handsome head, don't you think, Marsden?"

"It's murder," I said. I was horrified that he could talk about it so lightly.

"No. It's the way of the Borders. You'll have to get used to it. Now let's go on a hot trod after Nebless Clem, shall we?"

"What is this hot trod?" I asked.

"It means we chase him while he's still on the road. We hope to catch him with the cattle – and that's something the people up here call being caught 'red hand'. For a hot trod we carry the burning turf on the end of a lance. We can then cross the border and ride through Scotland till we catch our Reivers. And everyone has to help us, or be hanged if they refuse."

We mounted and clattered out of the castle courtyard, through the streets of Berwick and westwards into the hills, always following the lance with the burning turf. "They must have a few hours start," I said. "By the time the woman reached Berwick they'd be well into Scotland."

The Warden shook his head. "Cattle driving is a slow business. But sheep are worst of all. They'll be lucky to do a league in two hours. We'll catch them if we get on their trail."

Forster led the way across the wilderness of heather and bracken. Sometimes we climbed the rolling hills rather than take the long valley road around them. Sometimes we stopped in a village. A man in mudstained rags came out of his turf cottage to tell us, "Nebless Clem Croser and Evilwillit Sandie were leading about ten men and driving eight cattle. They crossed the stream at Bogells Beck."

"Good man," Forster said.

"Do I get a reward if you hang them?"

"One tenth of the stolen goods," Forster promised. "You'll get a cow." We spurred our horses along the track. Although the weather had been dry, the grass on the track was well trampled. Horses and cattle had passed that way in the last hour.

At the stream they called Bogells Beck the ground turned stony and we lost the trail. There were a few miserable huts huddled around a well. Men, women and children were working in the fields. I called to the nearest one, "Have you seen a gang of men driving cattle this way?"

A woman turned and looked at me as if I were quite out of my mind. "Men? Cattle?" she said in a strange accent. "No, sir. I've seen nothing."

"There's a reward," I promised.

"Aye," she nodded. "And what's the reward? The Reivers will come back and burn our houses while we're sleeping in them!"

"So you *have* seen them?"

"I've seen *nothing*," she said. Two small children who wore few clothes and no shoes clutched at her skirts and stared at me with hatred.

"Come on, Marsden!" Forster cried. "You're wasting time!"

"I thought these people might have seen something," I shouted back.

"Hah!" Forster roared. "These people are Scottish. We

crossed the border when we crossed Bogells Beck. They won't betray their Reiver friends, man."

"The law says they have to," I argued. "You can hang them for refusing to help a lawful pursuit."

Forster leaned across from his horse and slapped my shoulder.

"See many trees around here, Marsden?"

I looked across the stony fields to the hills covered in coarse grass and shale. A few threadbare sheep searched for scraps of something to eat. There was not enough soil for a tree to take root. "No."

"Exactly! There aren't enough trees to hang all the Scots who refuse to help a warden!" he laughed. "And the English do the same when the Scottish warden crosses the border to hunt for English thieves. London makes one set of laws. We live by another. That's your first lesson in Border law, my friend."

The path twisted and climbed over a steep pass. It suddenly grew narrow and the rocky walls were like a tunnel. As the road widened again at the other side, we came across a sweating group of ten weary cattle and a few sheep scattering into the hills around.

John Forster reined in his horse. He had been smiling and telling me about the area we were travelling through. Now his face turned pale. "Ready, men!" he cried. "It's a trap! Marsden, get your men ready to defend themselves!"

There was no one in sight. The only sound was the soft grate of swords being drawn, horses panting and the cattle complaining. They were stopped at the end of the narrow pass and blocking our way. Our group was too large to turn the horses around and go back the way we'd come.

Forster spoke quickly. "They've got two men at the far

end to hold the cattle in the pass like a stopper in a bottle. The rest of the gang have ridden back. They'll be above us with arrows and come from behind us with lances. We'll be picked off like pigs in a pen!"

He struggled in the swirling mass of horses to turn. Suddenly there was a scream. A signal. Four men appeared from behind the rocks above us. They held long-bows and crossbows and began firing. Bolts and arrows struck horses and riders. In the panic men fell and were trampled. There were soft cries of pain, but everyone stayed surprisingly quiet so they could hear the Warden's instructions. "Off your horses, men. Dismount!"

As he called this, the first of the Scots Reivers with lances rode into the narrow pass, threw their lances, spun round and raced away.

Still arrows rained down. If we sheltered under the rocky wall on the left, the archers on the right could pick us off. Warden Forster crouched down and ran after the riders who'd thrown their lances. The further we ran the further away we were from the deadly hail of arrows. A boulder at the English end of the pass sheltered us and about ten of our men. Four horsemen turned and faced us. "They'll come at us with their second lances," Forster said. "They won't throw them. They'll use them to stab. Be ready. Here they come."

The riders came towards us, their fierce faces grinning with the joy of facing Englishmen on foot with short swords to defend themselves. John Forster decided not to wait to be stabbed like a pig in the pen. He ran forward ten paces and stood in the middle of the road. "Clem!" he cried. "Surrender the cattle to us and go home."

The leading horseman nudged his horse forward a stride. His rust-bed beard was tangled and matted. A scar stretched from his right eye to the left corner of his mouth. Some sword stroke had also taken off half his nose. He showed strong yellow teeth in a grim smile. "If I kill you, Warden Forster, then I'll have the cattle and the fame!"

"If you kill me, King Henry will send an army to drag you to the gallows."

"Not if the army is stupid enough to fall into a simple trap like this," he roared back.

I stood at Forster's right shoulder. The Warden muttered, "He's right. I was so busy describing the pleasures of Border reiving, I forgot to think." He called across to the Scottish raiders, "Go home. Leave the cattle. And I'll forget this raid."

Nebless Clem's reply was to lower his lance and spur his horse forward. The Warden stood, legs apart, sword ready as the Reiver rushed towards him, spear pointed at his heart. When the point was an arm's length away Forster slashed at it and knocked the spear aside. But as the Scotsman rode past he swung the iron tip back and it clanged against the Englishman's steel bonnet.

The blow would have knocked many a man's head clean off his shoulders. Forster fell to his knees and dropped his sword. He shook his head and raised himself on to one knee, but the man with no nose had already swung the little pony round and changed his grip on the spear to stab downwards at the fallen warden.

John Forster raised a hand in a helpless gesture to brush the sharp point away. There was a strange silence in the air as every Englishman and Scot stopped fighting to watch the duel. Nebless Clem brought back his hand so he could stab with all the power in that tree-trunk arm.

And the silence was broken by the crack of a pistol. I

had pulled it out of my belt and fired at the Reiver's back. Those old wheel-lock pistols were hard to aim and the lead ball simply caught the Scot on the shoulder. But the noise was enough to startle the pony. It reared and threw the Reiver to the ground. In a moment I had drawn my knife and leapt on him. I held the knife to the man's throat and swung him round so he shielded me from his troop of thieves. "Throw down your weapons!" I cried.

The Scots didn't move. John Forster rose stiffly to his feet, pulled out his dagger and cut the leather reins from the pony. He quickly made a loop in the leather and threw it over Nebless Clem's neck. Then he tied the other end to the quivering pony. "Now, if I slap this pony it will gallop off and this Scots cow-dropping will be strangled to death. It's a slow way to die, but not as slow as starving to death. That's what would have happened to the woman you stole these cattle from, isn't it?"

Ten pairs of Scottish eyes glared silently at the Warden who turned to his own troop and asked, "Anyone killed?"

English soldiers walked out of the narrow pass clutching at bleeding wounds and one struggled to pull a sword from his leg. It seemed no one had been killed in the ambush. "You're lucky, Clem, my friend," Warden Forster said grimly. "Now, how about my offer? You leave quietly and I take the cattle back?"

"I'd have killed you if it hadn't been for yon rat-faced Englishman," the Reiver leader said, looking at me with eyes filled with poison.

"But you didn't."

"Using pistols is cheating," the Scotsman complained.

John Forster turned to me. "Slap the pony with your sword!"

I'd have done it happpily, but Clem cried, "No! No! I

never meant to steal the cattle. I just found them on the road! I was looking after them till someone claimed them!"

Forster shook his head. My sword was still raised to strike the pony and send the Reiver to Hell. "The woman described the thief. He had no nose. How many nebless people are there on the Borders, Clem?"

"At least ten!"

"How many?"

"Well, two that I know of."

"But the other one's dead," Forster sighed.

"He wasn't dead the last time I saw him alive," Clem said. He was sulking like a spoilt child.

The Warden unfastened the leather from the Reiver's neck. "Take your clothes off, Clem," he ordered.

"What?"

"You heard."

The Reiver slowly began to unfasten his armour till he was left with just his shirt and hose. "Now the rest of your men." In ten minutes the Reivers stood shivering on the mountainside while their armour lay in a pile at our feet.

Ten minutes after that the Scots were mounted and heading back north. Warden Forster called after them, "Hey! Evilwillit Sandie!"

The Scots captain stopped and turned. "What?"

"Give my love to Mary!"

The Reiver waved a hand and rode on. "Who's Mary?" I asked.

"My sister," Forster explained. "She married one of the Dixon family in his valley."

I felt angry and cheated. "Is that why you spared that Reiver's life? Because you're a friend of his family?"

Forster shrugged. "I spared his life because he might spare mine one day."

"But your job is to kill Scots!"

"No. My job is to protect English people and their homes and animals."

"But don't you hate them?" I asked.

"Why should I?"

"Because they're your enemy!"

"So are a dozen English villains." The Warden stopped and looked at me. "Do you hate Scots, Marsden?"

"Of course."

"Why?"

I thought about it. "Because they killed my father at Flodden."

"And wasn't your father trying to kill Scots at the same time? And weren't they just defending themselves?"

I had no answer to that. But I knew at that moment I hated an Englishman more than I'd ever hated a Scot. He was a traitor and his name was Warden John Forster.

Forster arranged for a sergeant to lead the wounded men and the stolen animals back to Berwick. Then he selected ten men. "Let's get this Scottish armour on, lads."

"Why?" I asked. "Where are we going?"

"Why, to carry out King Henry's orders. We're going to steal some cattle. Stir up trouble on the Borders."

I took off my plate armour and placed a dirty buff jack over my shirt. I climbed on to my pony and turned it to face north.

"This way, Marsden!" Forster cried.

"But that's the way to England," I said, puzzled.

"It is. And we're going to steal some English cattle. We'll have roast beef tonight!" he laughed. The Warden turned to ride south. I shook my head and followed.

CHAPTER TWELVE

"Something wicked this way comes"

My grandfather smiled at the memory, and old John Forster chuckled too. "You can see what John's plan was, can't you?"

I couldn't. But Hugh Richmond saved me by explaining. "Your men would steal English cattle while you were dressed as Scots. The English farmers would try to get their revenge by stealing Scottish cattle and the Scots would make their own raids and so it would go on!"

"That's right," Sir John Forster said. "We picked a farm owned by the powerful Charlton family in Northumberland. As we stole the cattle we cried, 'A Kerr! A Kerr!' then rode off north. Naturally the Scottish Kerr family got the blame. The Charltons attacked the Kerrs and the Kerrs attacked the Charltons and we had a full-scale feud on our hands. Then we stirred up trouble between the English Fenwicks and the Scots Elliots and we even turned the Scottish Elliots against the Scottish Kerrs."

Grandfather laughed. "King Henry had sent us to raid and reive. We didn't have to. We just had to light the fuse and watch the powder barrel explode. The King was delighted. Why, he even made plain John Forster into Sir John Forster."

"But people must have died in all these raids," I objected.

"They did," Sir John said, running a hand over his cropped hair. "But nowhere near the ten thousand that died at Flodden Field. King James V had so much trouble on his Borders he couldn't invade England even if he'd wanted to. Anyway, a lot of the ones who died were the cattle thieves and horse-stealers anyway."

We looked into the glowing fire in the room and wondered at the people who had died because Henry VIII had wanted to keep his Scottish neighbours busy. There was a knock at the door and a guard said that our meal was ready. Men brought in steaming plates and placed them on the table.

Hugh Richmond looked at the wooden dish in front of him and clutched a pale hand to his heart. "God's teeth! What is it?" he cried.

"It's a porridge with pieces of meat in it," Grandfather explained. "It's what most folk in the region eat – if they're lucky enough to have the meat, of course. A lot of the time they have to make do with the porridge by itself."

"But it's disgusting!" said the spy, twisting his handsome face into a mask of horror.

John Forster stuck a spoon into the mess and began to eat. I tried a little myself. It didn't taste very exciting, but I was hungry and it filled me. "Have you ever been hungry, Master Richmond?" the old soldier asked.

"Not hungry enough to eat horse food," the young man replied.

"Then I suggest you go back to Newcastle before you starve. The food you'll get between here and Berwick will only be worse."

Hugh pulled a large white piece of linen from his sleeve

and mopped at his brow. "I think I've died and gone to Hell," he whispered.

"If you think this is Hell then you've never been to the Borders," John Forster snorted. "And you never did tell me why you are here."

Hugh looked at Grandfather and I saw the old man give the slightest of nods as if to say Forster was to be trusted.

"I have a task from Queen Elizabeth's Secretary of State, Sir Robert Cecil himself. He is concerned that so many of Her Majesty's loyal subjects have been disappearing in the north. He thinks there is no point in sending an army to investigate. He thinks one man has a better chance of slipping across the border and finding the truth."

The old soldier scraped the last of the porridge from his bowl and said, "I've heard the stories. Of course I don't ride out any longer. I can't imagine how a troop of a hundred men or more can just disappear when they cross the border."

"They used to kidnap them in our day," Grandfather said.

"Aye," Forster agreed. "They'd hold them prisoner. But there was always a reason. And the reason was usually money. They would ask for ransom money before they set them free. It was against the law, of course – you can only ask for ransom if your enemy has been captured in a battle – but it has always gone on along the border."

"So they still do that, do they?" Hugh asked, eager to learn about the wild ways of this part of the country.

"They do. But, since Sir Clifford here left, they have discovered a new and easier way to make money," Sir John explained. "It's called 'black-meal' – though some call it black-mail. You know you can pay your rent in money or in corn meal? Well, gangs have been coming around and demanding an extra rent – an illegal, black rent. Black rent, black-meal, black-mail – call it what you want. The farmers pay the money or they have their farms destroyed. If they pay it, the gangs protect the farmer. It's just a vicious bully trick, every bit as cruel as the cattle raids. One man who refused to pay was burned over his own fire."

"But what's this got to do with the men who disappeared?" Hugh asked. He was so interested in the old man's description that he had dipped his spoon into his porridge and begun to eat without realizing it.

Forster nodded. "Good question. The government passed a law saying that in future black-meal will be punished by hanging. A party of law officers heard about a Scottish gang of black-mealers and followed them over the border to arrest them. That's when they disappeared."

"Are these gangs powerful enough to fight a hundred officers?" Hugh asked.

"It's possible, but I just can't believe it," Sir John sighed. "Black-mailers bully the weak. They run and hide from the strong. And another thing."

"What?" Hugh said. The spoon hung in the air between the bowl and his open mouth.

"There is another strange happening on the border."

This time I found myself drawn into the mystery. "What?" I breathed.

"There have been large cattle raids. Bigger raids than we've had for years. Heavily armed men have been riding into England and stealing herds of a hundred or more at a time. It's not the old family gangs that are doing it. It's new bands of strangers stealing far more than any village could eat in a hundred years! There's something hidden in those old hills. Something big and hungry and evil that's swallowing men and swallowing cattle. It's as if the Scots are trying to feed the belly of some monstrous dragon!"

"But there're no such things as dragons!" said Hugh Richmond worriedly.

Sir John waved his spoon at the spy and said, "Well, you'll find out soon enough, won't you?"

"Will I? How?"

"Because you're just a day's ride from the border. Leave tomorrow morning and you'll be filling the dragon's belly by tomorrow night. That's if you don't get lost in the maze of paths through the Cheviots, of course."

"Oh, but Sir Clifford Marsden has offered to be my guide."

Forster shook his head. "Sir Clifford has done well to bring you this far safely. It isn't fair to ask him to go any further."

"I want to go!" Grandfather said stubbornly. "I want to do one great deed before I die." He turned and looked with envy at his old enemy, who'd become his old friend. "You've done your great deed, John. You'll be remembered as long as history books are read."

Sir John wiped his mouth with a napkin and let his eyes drop modestly.

"What did you do?" I asked him.

"I saved Queen Elizabeth and all of England from defeat by her bitterest enemies," he said simply.

"Wonderful!" said Hugh Richmond. "Tell us more."

Sir John rose to his feet, walked to a sideboard and took a flagon of wine. He filled four wine cups and passed one to each of us. Grandfather took the poker from the fire and plunged it into his wine till it foamed and spat. He liked his wine warm before bed. "Mary, Queen of Scots was a Catholic," said Sir John. "And she was the centre of Catholic plots to kill Elizabeth and invite the Spanish to invade."

"They did that with their Armada in 1588," I said. Everyone knew the story of Sir Francis Drake and our defence against the invasion of the Spanish galleons.

"They did. But, thanks to Sir John Forster, we knew about their plans. We were prepared."

"What did you do, Sir John?" I asked.

He sipped his wine with some pleasure. I could see he enjoyed telling this story, and not for the first time. "I had my men on patrol, looking out for Reivers. They came across an old man travelling through the most deserted wastes of Northumberland and stopped him. If he'd told them some simple story they'd have let him go. He clearly wasn't a Reiver and he was no danger. But the foolish man refused to give his name, or say what he was doing there. They arrested him and brought him to me."

"He could still have got away with it, though," Grandfather said.

"We searched his baggage and found dentist's instruments, including a mirror. Nothing else. I knew I'd have to release him. Then the man made his second mistake. He offered me a bribe if I would let him go. I knew he must be hiding some terrible secret, but I had no idea what it was. So I looked at his instruments again. There was nothing there. Nothing!"

"But what about when you looked at the mirror again?" Grandfather said with a satisfied nod.

"Hidden between the mirror and its backing I found a paper. It was covered in writing in some secret code. I knew then that the man was a spy on his way from Scotland to the traitors in England. I sent the man and his letter to Elizabeth's spymaster, Sir Francis Walsingham, and his team cracked the code."

"England was saved," said Grandfather. "The whole country owes Sir John Forster a huge debt."

"What a marvellous story!" Hugh Richmond said.

Grandfather and Sir John exchanged a quick glance. Then Sir John said, "Why?"

"Why what?"

"Why is it a marvellous story?"

"Well, well, an enemy spy being caught by a Border warden. The whole country saved! Isn't that marvellous?" Hugh asked.

"Not if you're the spy," Grandfather said.

"Not if you're the spy," Hugh agreed.

"And what are you, Master Hugh?"

There was a silence in which we could hear the distant tramping of marching feet and someone shouting orders. Finally Hugh said quietly, "I'm a spy."

"And where will you be tomorrow at this time?"

"In an enemy country."

"And what will happen if you are caught?"

"I don't like to think."

"Then perhaps you should," Grandfather said. "It may make you more careful. Sir John here saved England by catching a spy; you could lose England by being caught as a spy."

The young man rose on shaking legs. "I think I'll go to bed, if you don't mind."

"Aren't you going to finish your supper?"

The spy pushed away his plate. He didn't even notice that he'd eaten most of the porridge. "I'm not hungry."

Sir John called for a guard to show Hugh Richmond into a tower room for the night. "Sleep well, Master Richmond!" he called into the darkening evening air. I didn't hear a reply.

Sir John returned to stir the fire into life. Grandfather said, "Lord Lambton says he's a clever young man."

Sir John snorted softly. "I can't see him growing to be a clever old man, like you and me, Clifford."

"We've done our best to prepare him," Grandfather sighed. "But you're right. I can't ride much further without a rest. Perhaps we could ride on to Berwick slowly. We could arrange to meet Hugh Richmond if he gets back across the border alive."

"He'll never do that if he goes alone," Sir John said.

"I agree. He needs someone sensible with him."

"I wish we could send someone we trust," Sir John said. "The men of Alnwick Castle all have long family roots that grow over the Borders. Henry VIII was right to send you and the Durham men back in the Thirties. You have no connections up here. You could be trusted. If only there were someone like you. But someone younger and fitter that we could trust."

"I only know one," Grandfather said.

"But will he go?" Sir John asked.

The wind moaned in the chimney like some lost and lonely ghost. "Of course I'll go," I said. And the two old men smiled.

CHAPTER THIRTEEN

"That tears shall drown the wind"

Long after Hugh Richmond went to bed we talked around the fireplace at Alnwick Castle. "You're a Marsden," my grandfather said seriously. "And for hundreds of years the Marsdens have hated the Scots. It's in our blood, boy."

Sir John Forster chuckled. "There was no one more fierce in fighting than your grandfather. He spent four years up here stirring up trouble. I've seen lots of Reivers and lots of Moss Troopers in my time. But not many enjoyed their work as much as Clifford Marsden."

"They killed my father at Flodden," Grandfather said. "I never forgot that."

"And they killed some of my best friends in fighting too, but I never learned to hate them the way you do," said Sir John. "I enjoyed the thrill of the fight and the joy of creating mischief. I never took it seriously."

"I suppose that's why you and I didn't like one another in those days," Grandfather sighed. "We were very different." He swung round to look at me. "It's easy to hate someone when you know they hate you. But I never did understand King Henry. I never knew a man so full of hatred. It burned inside him like a blacksmith's forge. And when the King hated, people died."

"Tell him about Solway Moss," Sir John urged.

Grandfather nodded. "Yes. If you're going across the border, you need to know. The Scots have long memories. They remember Flodden when we killed their king. But they also remember Solway Moss where we came back and defeated his son – James V. We even killed his granddaughter Mary, Queen of Scots. No wonder the Marsdens are worried that James VI will take the English throne and let the Scots have their revenge."

"Tell him about Solway Moss," his old friend repeated.

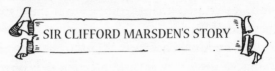

SIR CLIFFORD MARSDEN'S STORY

James V was a sad man. He had a thin, worried face half hidden by a dark wispy beard. He came to the throne when he was only a year and a half old, and he never had any peace. Scottish lords were fighting and killing each other to control the boy king. When he grew up he needed an army to take control of his own throne.

And all the time King Henry VIII was trying to make problems for him. Our troublemaking on the border was exhausting for James V. Worse than a real war, in fact.

His first queen died after they'd been married just seven months; then both young sons from his second marriage died in a year. And did fat King Henry take pity on James? What do you think?

Henry wanted to attack France again. And every time England attacks France, then Scotland attacks England. Henry had to keep Scotland quiet. Henry was always afraid of being stabbed in the back.

I had ridden home to Marsden Manor with my men after four years of tormenting the Border Scots. John

Johnston the steward was full of the news from the south as soon as I entered the main hall.

"We've heard that James is making treaties with the French again and with the Spanish. They say he is planning to invade England."

"The King must be pleased," I told him. "It'll give us the chance to smash the Scots once and for all."

"We've heard that our king wants to meet James."

I nodded. "He'll want to bully the man. You know, Johnston, it's strange that in thirty years these two kings have never met."

Johnston nodded eagerly. "Messengers to James V stopped here on their way north. It's no secret. King Henry said, 'Meet me in York at the end of September!' They even say that the northern leaders will be going to the meeting too. Does that mean us, sire?"

"I'd think so. And, since you've cared for Marsden Manor so well while I've been away, I'll take you with me."

John Johnston was thrilled by the idea of seeing the King again. He remembered the brilliant young man who'd secretly visited Marsden Manor thirty years before. He was going to be disappointed.

Now a man like Henry VIII couldn't have a nice quiet meeting, could he? No, he had to make this trip a grand procession. That was bad news for his prisoners in the Tower of London. If the King was leaving London, then he didn't want traitors plotting as soon as he turned his back. He had them all executed. Why, he even had the old Countess of Salisbury executed. Her only crime was being the mother of a man who supported the Pope. The King wasn't bothered about trials. He just had her neck put on the block while some useless boy hacked her head off very clumsily.

Blood, blood. Henry always had to have blood. And

gold. He was going to show his might to the people of England.

He took a thousand knights and stopped off at cities along the way. And everywhere he stopped he changed into a suit made from cloth of gold.

For fat old Henry had something new to show his people. Henry had a beautiful young queen, Katherine Howard. Anne Boleyn had lost her head to the sweep of a French sword and his next queen, Jane Seymour, had died soon after their son was born. He'd married Anna of Cleeves when he saw her lovely portrait then divorced her soon after he saw her in the flesh.

I never saw Jane or Anna of Cleeves, but I did see Katherine. I went with the other northern lords to join Henry in York. We stayed in the fields outside the city walls where two hundred tents shone with every colour of cloth that the dye-makers could produce. It was more colourful than the march to Flodden nearly thirty years before. From the town walls the tents looked like a field of flowers. All that beauty for one ugly man.

We went up to the castle to meet the King. In the great hall we knelt down while trumpets sounded and he was carried in. His swollen face was blotched pink behind the grizzled beard, and the mean little mouth hung open as he gasped and struggled to a throne that had been placed on a platform at the end of the hall. He was fifty years old now, and men no longer talked about what would happen "if" the King died. Now they talked about "when" he died.

The girl alongside him was tiny and fragile, but she was also lively and found it hard to sit still while her monstrous husband panted out his message to us. "Our nephew James will arrive tomorrow. I want every man dressed in full armour and ready for battle. We are not going to kill our nephew, of course. But we are going to frighten him into signing this peace with us," he said, waving a piece of parchment. He chuckled at the thought and the effort of laughing made him gasp. Katherine turned and held his hand till he had recovered.

There was a stir at the doorway behind the throne and a messenger in the green and white Tudor colours hurried in, knelt in front of the King, and handed him a message which the King read. As he read the pink blotches of his face turned to purple. Henry VIII had always had a high voice. Now it was almost a screech. "It seems," he puffed, "it seems that our nephew does not trust us! He is refusing to come south of his border to meet us." His wheezing was so loud that I could hear him breathing even though I was thirty paces away. "If James will not come to us, then we will have to pay a visit to him. My Lord of Norfolk!" he called.

The Duke walked forward and knelt before the King. "Your Majesty," he said.

"We will make plans to teach this Scottish puppy a lesson."

Henry struggled to his feet while his tiny queen looked anxious. He stood with his legs apart so that he was steadier, and rested a hand on his dagger. "Remember Flodden, my lords. When I attack France again you will attack Scotland again. Go home. Train your men. Wait for the order."

He managed to walk from the hall with the help of the young Queen's uncle, the Duke of Norfolk. As the door closed behind him the men in the hall all began talking at once. "War," John Johnston said, his face twisted with pain.

"Yes, war!" I cried. "After years of sticking pins into our Scottish friends I can meet them in a real battle."

The room quietened as men hurried out to spread the news and make preparations. "What's wrong, Johnston man?" I cried to my steward.

"I was at Flodden," he said soberly. "I saw your father die. I don't want to watch you die."

"You're too old to go, Johnston," I said. I stupidly thought it was fear for his own life that made him so gloomy. Now I know it was fear for Marsden Manor. I had no children of my own to take over if I did get killed. I didn't listen to the man.

"The King's too old, but he'll be going off to France," said John Johnston. "I hope the young Queen doesn't lose a husband in war the way your mother did."

A soft voice spoke behind us. "The young Queen has more to lose than a husband."

We turned and I saw a face I'd seen five years before, but had never forgotten. I remembered the lady-in-waiting to Anne Boleyn. "Eleanor!" I said. "It's good to see you again."

"And you, Master Marsden."

"Are you still with the royal court even though ..."

"Even though Anne Boleyn was murdered by the King?" she asked, raising an eyebrow. She was amused to see how shocked I was when she used the word "murder".

"Yes. I thought Anne's friends would have been in disgrace after her execution," I said.

"I'm a friend of the Norfolk family," she said. I noticed that she had fine grey eyes that sparkled even in the gloom of the castle hall. "When Katherine married the King, she invited me to go back with her. I knew Hampton Court and the King and how to look after a queen."

"It's strange that you knew both queens," I said.

Eleanor looked at me curiously. "No, it isn't," she said. "After all, Anne Boleyn and Katherine Howard were cousins."

"Were they?" I said stupidly, blushing at my ignorance. "I've spent a lot of time on the Scottish Borders. I don't know much about London happenings."

Eleanor didn't seem to notice my clumsy explanation. "I want to talk to you," she said quietly.

"Yes?"

She looked at our steward. "Alone. It is extremely secret," she said.

John Johnston held up a hand and said, "I need to return to the tent to prepare for the evening meal. Excuse me." He gave me a wink and walked away quickly.

Eleanor took my hand and led me to a bench that stood against the wall. She lifted the tapestry and glanced behind it.

"Is it really so very secret?" I laughed.

The young woman didn't smile. "Katherine Howard is a foolish child," she said.

"She is very beautiful," I said. I was not used to the ways of women. I'd spent too long in the company of men.

"Beauty is no use if a woman has no brain," she snapped.

"Of course not," I said.

She tugged at a strange-looking collar around her neck. It was a ruff, of course, but it was a new fashion in that year and I'd never seen one before. "Katherine is married to the King and the King is a very jealous man. She is also being very, very friendly with a man of her own age, one of the King's most trusted servants a man called Thomas Culpeper. Every night that we've been away from London,

Queen Katherine has been having secret meetings with Culpeper."

I suddenly felt cold. Anne Boleyn had been accused of the same crime and Henry had shown no mercy. "I see," I said.

"Everybody now knows about Katherine and Culpeper."

"Everybody except the King."

Eleanor nodded, her grey eyes serious and sad. "There are so many jealous people. Someone may tell the King tonight. They may wait until next week or next month, but they won't wait forever. One day he will find out."

"And Katherine's pretty head will roll like her cousin's," I said grimly.

"Not only Katherine's head. Culpeper will die. And so will all the people who helped Katherine and Culpeper to meet. Lady Rochford is encouraging the meetings and I serve Lady Rochford."

"Lady Rochford will die," I said.

Eleanor leaned forward. "And so will I."

"That's not fair! Can't you do anything about it?"

"I can leave the Queen's service now. Tonight. This very moment before someone tells Henry about Culpeper."

"Won't the King and Queen want to know why you are leaving so suddenly?"

"Of course."

"So what will you tell them?"

"That I have met a man whom I first met in London, and I am staying in the north to marry him."

I nodded. "Good idea. Who is this man?"

Eleanor turned her large grey eyes on me, closed her lips firmly, raised one fine eyebrow and waited.

"Do I know him?" I asked.

The only reply I got was for the other eyebrow to lift. Then I felt a trickle of cold sweat run from the back of my neck down my spine. My mouth fell open a little. Eleanor gave one small nod of her head.

"Me?"

Her lips curved slightly upwards. "You'd only have to pretend."

I thought about it. "No," I said. "I can't lie to my king. That is treason."

Her eyes showed a flicker of disappointment. "I understand," she said. "It was too much of me to ask."

I took a deep breath and felt the cold sweat sticking my shirt to my back. "I mean I will marry you – but I won't just pretend to marry you."

We have been married for more than half our lives, but that is almost the only time I have seen Eleanor's eyes fill with tears.

That night she told me the King wished to see me. I knelt in front of him as he sat next to his lively, treacherous young queen. I remembered that he didn't want his subjects to look him in the face. I kept my eyes half lowered.

"So, you're taking our Eleanor away from us, are you?" he grunted.

"Yes, Your Majesty."

"She's a fine woman," he said.

"Indeed, Your Majesty."

"Not so fine as my Queen Katherine," he said with a rumbling laugh that ended in a deep cough. "But I wish you as much happiness with her as I have found with my queen."

Oh, God, I prayed to myself. I hope not!

"And I hope she will be as happy as I am," Katherine giggled. "Though no other woman could have a man who is a god on earth," she sighed, looking lovingly at the monstrous old man. From my kneeling position I could smell the festering wounds and see the stains seeping through the white hose that covered his bloated legs.

"One thing before you go, Marsden," the King said.

"Your Majesty?"

"Pass me your sword."

He took the blade from me and lowered it on to each shoulder. "Arise Sir Clifford Marsden!"

I rose, shaking, to my feet. "Thank you, Your Majesty. I can never repay you ..."

"You can," he said. His voice was hard as that blade now. "You have done good work on the Borders. But there'll be a bigger test soon. Are you ready for it?"

"For war with Scotland, Your Majesty? I'm ready for it. I have been since they killed my father at Flodden."

"Revenge," Henry said. "Revenge. What better feeling is there in the world? I wish I could be up there fighting alongside you. I hate the Scots more than I hate the French. I don't want you to beat them. I want you to destroy them. Do you understand, Marsden? Show no mercy, take no prisoners. I have waited nearly thirty years to do the job my half-witted queen should have done at Flodden. James died at Flodden and I wish I had held the sword that cut him down. I hope you're a man to do the same to his son in the next battle."

He was leaning over me, his stinking breath hot in my face. I had thought no one hated the Scots more than I did. Now I almost felt sorry for them.

CHAPTER FOURTEEN

"When the battle's lost and won"

As my grandfather paused in his story, his friend shook his head. Sir John Forster picked up a heavy log and threw it into the glowing ashes of the fire so that sparks showered upwards and on to the hearth. "You were supposed to be telling the boy about the battle, you old fool. He doesn't want to hear some old love story. You say she's still alive and you're still married?"

Grandfather nodded.

"Unlike pretty little Katherine Howard," Forster snorted.

Grandfather nodded. "Aye. Eleanor was right. Four weeks after they left York, Henry heard about Katherine and Culpeper. First he raged and then he wept because life had given him five worthless wives. Katherine wept too. They say she ran through the corridors of Hampton Court to plead for her life. He refused to see her."

"I have heard that her ghost still runs screaming through those same corridors," Forster said.

"Who can blame her? The axe is a cruel way to end your life. Especially when you're just twenty years old."

"What about Culpeper?" I asked.

"Oh, he died much more slowly and painfully. The King made sure of that," Grandfather explained.

"Henry liked his revenge," Forster nodded.

"So did his armies kill James V?" I asked.

"It's a strange thing. In fact the whole invasion was strange. The English were fired up by King Henry's hatred. Norfolk led thirty thousand men across the border and burned everything they found north of the border. But James wasn't such a vicious man and that seemed to affect the Scots. They didn't fight as bravely for their king as they could do."

"If you don't tell him about Solway Moss, then I will," John Forster said. He scooped grey ash from the fire and spread it over the hearth, and used the poker to draw a map of the battle. I smiled because back at Marsden Manor my Great-Uncle George told stories of battles in the same way. "The Duke of Norfolk went through Alnwick here and up the east coast. Then he marched inland and started destroying Scottish towns. He burned a dozen towns, then marched back to Berwick."

"He ran out of beer," Grandfather said.

"What?" I laughed.

"Beer! An army can't survive without beer. Norfolk didn't have enough to get his men to Edinburgh, so he turned back."

"Make sure you take plenty of beer with you when you leave tomorrow," Sir John warned me.

"I think Hugh Richmond only drinks wine," I said.

"Then he'll die of thirst," Grandfather sniffed.

John Forster drew a new line in the ashes. "While Norfolk was burning Scotland to the west of Berwick, your grandfather and I were here in Carlisle. Right over in the west. James decided it would be a good idea to invade in the west. All that stood in the way of his eighteen thousand soldiers was our troop of three thousand."

"We didn't have a chance," Grandfather said.

"You were beaten?" I asked.

Grandfather straightened his back and looked at me with mock disgust. "Certainly not! We won!"

"How?" I gasped.

"Because we had three thousand men with one leader Warden Wharton. The Scots had eighteen thousand men with no real leader."

"They had King James."

"James fell ill and stayed behind. He sent the army on to meet us and stupidly forgot to tell them who was in charge," Grandfather explained. "They had no trouble marching through the English valleys, burning the families out of their cottages. That's what the Reivers in the Scottish army were good at. But we didn't just sit in Carlisle Castle and wait for them to arrive and burn us out. We collected our three thousand men and set off to meet them."

"It was like meeting old friends," John Forster sighed. "A lot of the thieves from the Borders were in the front rows. We were close enough to call out greetings."

"And threats," Grandfather added. "I remember seeing Nebless Clem. He shouted, 'I've a score to settle with you, Marsden. You'll not be cheating by shooting me in the back this time. And I'll be eating dinner in Marsden Hall tomorrow night!' I laughed at him. It's strange, but I wasn't afraid. The years on the Borders had toughened me. The sight of an armed Scotsman didn't disturb me."

"Did you fight him, Grandfather?" I asked.

"We came closer. Close enough for me to see the scar across his ugly face," the old man said. "Neither of us had bothered to draw our weapons. We were waiting for orders to start the attack. It was a cold day and it kept us warm, shouting across at the Scots. Between ourselves we were wondering why the huge Scots army didn't just march forward and trample us into the frozen ground. Then Nebless Clem called, 'You'll have the rest of your army on the far side of the hill, have you?'"

John Forster nodded his cropped grey head eagerly and cut in, "We didn't stop to think about it! I shouted back, 'Yes, Clem, but there are only another ten thousand there.' It was a lie! A hopeless lie told in a hopeless situation. But no sooner had I said it than every Scot seemed to take a step backwards."

Grandfather took up the story. "What we didn't know was that Sir James Sinclair had told the other Scottish lords that he was in charge. And they all argued that he wasn't! Someone ordered the Scots cannon to fire, but they did very little damage. Warden Wharton gave the signal for us to draw our weapons and move forward it was no use waiting to be shot down. But still no one gave the Scots the order to move forward."

"So what did they do?" I asked.

"They stepped backwards. It's a natural thing to do. The men behind couldn't see what was happening and they stepped back in a bit more of a panic. The ones at the very back were running for their lives in five minutes."

"Aye, and it cost them their lives," Sir John said. "They ran into the River Esk and far more drowned than we ever killed. The nobles started surrendering to us. We captured two hundred of them and another thousand soldiers."

"We won a battle without fighting," Grandfather said, with a shake of his head. "All because of a little lie and a careless Scottish king."

I was tired now and the warmth of the fire was making me sleepy. But there was something worrying me. "I thought King James V died in battle like his father had at Flodden."

"Oh, no," Sir John said. "James died as a result of the battle. They took the news of the dreadful defeat to him. He was ill before. The news of the disaster drove him into his sick bed. And he never recovered. He died three weeks later."

Grandfather looked at me. "Wise doctors say a man can't die of a broken heart. They're wrong, William, lad. The shame of that battle at Solway Moss killed the King of Scotland."

The Marsden family didn't tell stories so they could boast about their great deeds. They told them so the younger ones could learn lessons. I knew I had to work out the lesson from the Solway Moss story, tired as I was. "The Scots aren't monsters. They're just human. We're scared of them, but they are just as scared of us."

"They are."

"And if we stand up to them no matter how weak we are we may just win through."

"We will. You're a boy and Hugh Richmond is a peacock. But go into Scotland with courage and anything is possible," Grandfather said. "The English lied about the extra ten thousand troops. Hugh Richmond is an actor whose job it is to deal with lies and illusions. Troops of two hundred men have failed to discover the secret across the border. I'm letting you go because I honestly believe you can do better." He smiled and stretched a hand out to ruffle my hair. "I wish I was going with you."

I went to bed and dreamed of walking across a border stream and meeting a Scottish Reiver. As I drew my sword to fight him, he raised his hands and lifted his head from his shoulders. The head turned into the head of a beautiful queen and it was screaming, "Henry, don't kill me! Oh, Henry, don't kill me." When I looked closely she had the face of our kitchen maid, Meg. Perhaps it was the ghost of poor little Katherine Howard wandering through this world. Perhaps I was just haunted by my own fear.

My grandfather gave me advice while I tried to eat breakfast. I was too excited at the thought of the journey ahead to be hungry. My head was too full of dreams and fears to listen to his words. I simply wanted to be on horseback and on the road. I pushed pieces of egg around my plate and said, "Yes, Grandfather," for the tenth time.

"You're not even listening."

"I am!" I objected.

"What did I just say?"

"You were telling me about a toy – I think."

"If I wasn't so stiff I'd take the flat of my sword to you," he growled. "I said boy, not toy. We are being followed by a boy. Now that you don't have an old man dragging you back like an anchor you should be able to outride him."

"Go across the moors and not along the main roads," John Forster advised. "You'll lose him easily once you reach the moors."

"Won't we lose ourselves?" I worried.

Hugh Richmond laughed. "No chance of that, young Will. I have a sense of direction like a homing pigeon!"

"Aye, that'll be because you have the brain of a homing pigeon," Grandfather muttered. Hugh smiled happily at the insult, thinking it was a joke. I knew Grandfather better.

John Forster gave us supplies of beer, bread, cheese and

dried beef. He also gave us a map. "Head north-west, just follow the River Aln from here," he said. "You'll come to the village of Eslington, then Windy Gyle. That's on the Scottish side of the border so be careful. And that's where the men have been disappearing."

"I'll know what to do when we get there," Hugh said.

"What will that be, Master Richmond?" Grandfather asked. "Tell them you're an English spy and ask what the Scots are doing with our men?"

Hugh grinned. "You are a wit, Sir Clifford. But we agents of the Queen never reveal our secret plans. Not even to our friends."

Half an hour later we were out of the town and winding our way up the valley of the Aln. "Can you tell me our secret plan now?" I asked.

Hugh let go of his reins and threw his hands into the air. "Haven't got one, Will! I thought I'd get to Eslington and ask the locals. Then we'll probably ride over the border and spy around a bit."

"So we're heading into deadly danger and you haven't got a plan?"

"That's about it. In the theatre we call it improvisation. The script is the plan – when it goes wrong, or when someone forgets their lines, then we sort of make it up as we go along," he said happily.

I thought about this as we guided our ponies through a dense wood that came down to the stony edge of the river. "What happens if the script goes wrong in the theatre, Hugh, and if you can't think of any way out of it?"

"The whole play stops. That happened once when Romeo fell off the stage and broke his leg in Mr Shakespeare's play."

"And what happens to the actors?"

"The audience may get upset and throw fruit at us."

"And if things go wrong in Scotland, Hugh? Do you think the Scots will just throw fruit at us?"

A troubled look crossed his face for a moment. "Probably not."

"If this secret of theirs is so great, they may kill us to keep it quiet."

"Probably, Will."

"So, wouldn't it be a good idea to have a plan? I mean, it's not exactly like being on stage, is it? People don't really die on stage."

Hugh laughed. "Mr Shakespeare says, 'All the world's a stage, and all the men and women merely players.'"

"Hugh!" I cried. "This isn't a play. You heard Grandfather's stories. The Reivers have a dozen ways of killing their enemies. They drop them into deep holes filled with water – murder holes they call them. They cut them into pieces. They shut them in their homes and set fire to them. What they don't do is throw fruit at them!"

"Trust me, Will. Trust me."

The trouble was I was beginning to doubt him. I trusted Grandfather. He'd been here before, faced all the dangers and survived. I wished he were still with us.

We climbed away from the river for a mile and reached the crest of a hill. Ahead of us the dull purple Cheviots rolled away under a cold, grey ceiling of cloud. I looked back to the east where the sun was shining and making the sea sparkle in a silver ribbon.

And I could see a small figure on a pony coming out of the riverside wood we'd just left. It was one of the ponies I'd bought from Wat Grey back in Marsden Village. The rider was a boy in a broad flat cap. "I don't suppose you've got a plan to deal with him?" I asked.

"Like Sir Clifford said, outride him," Hugh answered, and kicked his pony forward down the slope of the hill.

"There's a copse of trees ahead," I said, as I jogged after him. "Remember the old Reiver trick? Pretend to run away, hide, and wait and ambush the ones who're following you?"

"What would we do if we caught him?" Hugh asked, pressing on still faster.

"Make him tell us who he is and why he's following us."

"And if he refuses?"

"Torture him."

"Ugh!" Hugh cried. "What a crude idea. We might hurt the poor lad! He's probably some insignificant Scottish spy. And if we were caught we wouldn't want to be tortured, would we?" He kicked his pony into a gallop and I struggled to keep up with him.

As we reached a stretch of high moorland heather I was able to pull alongside him. "Where are we going, Hugh? We've lost the river!"

"It's down there behind that boulder," he said. "Keep the sun on your left and we can't go wrong."

"But the sun is behind clouds up here."

"True, but I can sense exactly where it is."

"Like a homing pigeon?"

"Exactly. We'll be in Eslington in two hours – and we'll have lost our Scottish spy by then."

Two hours later we were on high, bleak uplands where the grey skies melted into the grey rocks. Crows circled overhead as if they were waiting for us to die so they could pick out our eyes. My grandmother enjoyed singing an old northern ballad about three crows who did that to a dead knight. The only colour in the world was the yellow moss that clung here and there to the rock. We ate some cheese and bread while Hugh told me tales of the theatres in London. He was as cheerful as ever.

"I want to be an actor," I told him. "I saw some travelling players in Durham last year."

"I'll teach you some of Mr Shakespeare's speeches. Or Kit Marlowe's! I once played Doctor Faustus," he said, jumping to his feet. "'Ah, Faustus!'" he cried, so that his voice boomed and echoed off the cold rock. "'Now you have but two bare hours to live, and then you will be damned forever!'"

"Cheerful," I muttered, worried that I might really have but two bare hours to live if we didn't get out of this high cold desert of a place. I stood up. "Maybe we should head back down and find the river again," I suggested.

"Good idea, Will. I was just going to say the same thing myself," he said, mounting his pony.

A narrow gully led us down to a deep valley that seemed to be running westwards the way we wanted to go. The lower we went the more grass we could see growing through the moss and heather. Scrawny sheep picked their way around boulders, but scattered when we came too near.

At the bottom of the valley a stream splashed noisily over a pebble bed. A blackened skeleton of a house overlooked the stream. Once there had been a wall around a field at the back of the house. Now the wall was crumbling and purple-pink weeds were smothering whatever crops had grown there. "Fireweed," I said. "It grows wherever there's been a fire."

Somehow this deserted shell of a house was lonelier than the empty hills above. We followed a worn sheep trail up the valley and climbed a small ridge to get a better view of the way ahead. The air was clear and still here and we could see smoke rising about two miles ahead.

"Eslington!" Hugh cried. "I told you that you could trust me."

"You did," I smiled.

It was the last time I smiled for a few days. It was also the last time I'd place my trust in another person. Ever.

CHAPTER FIFTEEN

"Upon the next tree thou shalt hang alive"

The woman was as thin and grey as the smoke from her chimney. She had a brown sack hung round her neck and she was throwing seeds on to a poor patch of ground. A child followed behind using a rake to cover the seeds with soil and to chase away the screaming gulls that swooped and circled round her.

"Good evening!" Hugh called cheerfully to her.

The woman opened her mouth to reply, then seemed to change her mind. She pulled the child close to her and gave the smallest of nods. I guessed she was about thirty years old, but her stringy, colourless hair was already streaked with grey.

Hugh looked at the wood and turf huts that stood in an uneven line along the road. "So this is Eslington, is it?"

The woman's eyes flickered as if she were agreeing.

"Sorry, madam, have you lost your voice?" Hugh asked.

She pointed to her throat and nodded.

"I see," said Hugh. "I wonder if you'd like to earn a little money."

This time the nod was quite clear.

"I'll pay a silver groat for me and one for the boy here if you can give us shelter for the night."

The woman gave a sly smile and crooked a dirty finger

for us to follow her. We dismounted and walked behind her through the village. The cottages had no glass windows, only cracked shutters over holes in the turf walls. Through the doorways I could see the dull glow of turf fires, but very little furniture. Straw in the corner seemed to be for sleeping on. Sheepskins were the only bedclothes.

I was sure her home would be no better. Silent children clutched at hens and dogs as if we'd come to steal them. Grim-faced men and women watched wide-eyed as we led our ponies past their doors. At last we reached a larger building at the end of the village. Dogs guarded the building; not watchdogs, but small ratting dogs that would protect the building from the four-legged thieves who would come to steal the corn inside. This was the village grain store.

At one end there was a wooden wall that held the villagers' pathetic supply of corn for the winter. At the other end there were piles of hay that would feed the animals. The woman pointed.

"Looks warm and dry enough!" Hugh grinned. He reached into his leather purse and took out two groats. The woman gave a thin smile as he passed them over to her, but did not take her eyes off his face. "You are doing your queen a great service," Hugh said. "I will report to London how generous the people of Eslington have been."

"Hugh," I said out of the side of my mouth. "Remember what Grandfather said about these Border people. They marry people from Scotland. This woman might have relatives over the border. She might betray us. Be careful what you say."

"I am an actor," he said, "I study people. I understand people. This woman is as honest as the road to London is long." He turned towards her. "You are loyal to your country, aren't you, my friend?"

This time she nodded vigorously. She took the horses from us and helped us to unsaddle them. We carried our saddle packs into the barn and put them in a corner. "Now," Hugh said. "I need to talk to the local landowner. I have a few questions to ask about some men who have disappeared."

The woman jerked a thumb over her shoulder. She pointed to a solid stone tower that stood on the top of a small hill about half a mile outside the village. A wall ran round the outside and baskets of wood were placed at each corner ready to be lit as warning beacons. One for a small raid, two for a fast-moving raid and four for a large force of Reivers, I remembered.

"We'll go and see the landowner now, shall we?" Hugh suggested.

The woman shook her head and pointed a thin dirty finger at her chest.

"I think she's saying that she'll go and get him," I said.

She nodded and pointed for us to go back inside the barn. "We can have a bite to eat while we wait," Hugh said. "With any luck the landowner will offer us supper when he learns we are agents of the Queen. He may even offer us a more comfortable bed!"

As Hugh bent to pick up his saddle bag a sudden darkness came over the barn. The woman had swung the door shut. I hurried across and found she was placing a bar through iron loops. I pushed a shoulder against it, but we were fastened in.

"She's taken us prisoner!" I cried.

Hugh laughed. It seemed nothing could dull his good spirits. "Probably for our own protection. She knows we have money and doesn't want us to be robbed by the other poor villagers."

"How will locking us in stop us being robbed?" I asked.

Hugh tapped the side of his nose. "You'll see," he said.

The last of the autumn daylight spilled through cracks in the door frame, and I put an eye to one of them. The woman was hurrying along the road towards the tower. She stopped and started talking to a man.

"She can talk!" I said. "Why didn't she talk to us?"

"Shy," Hugh said.

She went on her way, while the man strode into the village. He was back a minute later, carrying a long pole with a wicked axe head on the top. "There's a man on guard outside the door," I said.

"See!" Hugh cried. "I told you they'd protect us!"

"But his pike!" I said.

"What about it?"

"It's twice the height of a man."

"Ah, yes, the good old English billhook. Much longer than the Scottish one. That's how we wiped them out at Flodden, you know. We used longer pikes. The Scots couldn't get near us with their shorter pikes."

"Couldn't they?" I said.

"Didn't you listen to a thing your grandfather told you?" Hugh sighed. "Here, take this beer," he said, handing me a pewter tankard.

"What's floating in it?" I asked.

"Dried beef. It'll soften up in the beer," he said, winking. "Old soldier's trick."

"You aren't a soldier," I reminded him. "You're an actor."

"Old actor's trick then. Makes the beef chew better."

"But it's salt beef. It makes the beer taste awful!"

"Look, Will, agents in the service of Her Majesty can't whine about the hardships we have to face. Just eat it."

Hugh was beginning to irritate me. He was good to listen to when he was talking about the theatre. But I was starting to realize that he was just acting out a new role – he was pretending to be a war hero. The trouble was that the man at the door wasn't using a pretend pike. If we tried to get out, then Hugh would find that we weren't in a play.

I chewed at the awful meat and longed for a plateful of the food I'd have been eating at Marsden Manor. Sometimes Meg put a thumb in the food as she served it. I'll swear she did it just to annoy me. I wouldn't have minded being served by Meg right then – thumb and all.

Other villagers were gathering outside the door now, and some of the children were pressing grubby faces against the cracks to see if they could get a better view of their strange visitors. Finally they scattered as a man arrived at the door and jumped down from his horse.

I stood back from the door and waited beside Hugh as the bar slid back and the door creaked open. The man who stood there was like something from my worst nightmare. He was tall and broad-shouldered. He wore a leather jack that I knew was filled with steel plates. His helmet was brightly polished and a peak shaded his face.

It was the face that shocked me most. It was a very old face with deep wrinkles around the eyes and mouth. His beard had once been rust-red, but it was grey now. The brown and weathered face might have been handsome at one time, but it was spoiled by an ancient scar that stretched from his right eye to the left corner of his mouth. Most frightening were the two nostrils that looked huge in the twisted stump of flesh that had once been a nose.

I didn't need to be told the man's name. There couldn't be two men who looked like Nebless Clem Croser.

As a villager swung the door open, the old Reiver chief stood in the doorway with a pistol in each hand.

"Welcome to Scotland," he said.

Hugh laughed. "Eslington isn't in Scotland, my friend."

The man's eyes narrowed suspiciously. He wondered if Hugh were making fun of him. Hugh reached inside his jerkin and the man shouted, "If you pull out that gun, you'll be carried back to England feet first!"

Hugh ignored him and pulled out his map. He stepped forward. "Look!" he said, pointing at the map. "Here we are. Can you read?"

"Aye."

"There's England, there's the border and there's Eslington. Eslington's in England!"

"I know that!" the man replied angrily. "But you're not in Eslington. You crossed the border at the burn with the burnt-out cottage. This is Windy Gyle and you're in Scotland."

"Ha! Ha! Ha! Ha! Ha!" Hugh laughed crazily. "That old fool Forster needs a few lessons in map-drawing. We're twenty miles away from where we should be."

Nebless Clem Croser stepped forward and poked a pistol at Hugh. "Forster, you say? Were you sent here by John Forster?"

"You know him?" cried Hugh, as if it were a delightful surprise.

"Forster has burned more Scots homes than there are rats in England. I've a mind to send you back to him in fifty pieces!"

Hugh looked bewildered. His talent for "making it up" seemed to have deserted him. I stepped forward. "We stopped off at Alnwick last night. We met Sir John in Alnwick Castle. But he didn't send us. We're on our way to Scotland to entertain King James. We hear he's very fond of the theatre."

"The theatre?" Clem asked. "You're actors?"

"Of course!" Hugh said. "Surely you didn't think we were spies or something, did you ... ouch! Why did you kick my shin, Will?"

"We're actors," I said quickly.

"The woman said you told her you were in the service of the Queen," Clem said.

"I didn't know the woman could talk!" Hugh blinked.

"She can talk all right. She just didn't want you to hear her Scots accent, man. She has a lot more sense than some folk round here," he added, staring hard at the actor.

"I see!" Hugh smiled. "Well, I suppose mistakes do happen. If you won't let us go to see your king, then I suppose we'll just have to go back to England."

He began to walk past the old Reiver and out of the barn door. The man with the pike – the long Scottish pike, I remembered now – barred his way. Hugh spoke again and I wished I'd had that pike. I'd have seen just how much of that long wooden shank would go down his throat. For he said, "Sir Clifford Marsden will not be pleased if he finds you've held his grandson against his will!"

Nebless Clem sucked air noisily through the black holes in the middle of his face. "Marsden, you say?" He looked at me with new interest. "It was a Marsden that shot me in the back once. Cowardly thing to do, that. I've waited more than sixty years for my revenge," he said. "Sixty years! Now I can invite him to see his grandson hanging by the neck from the walls of my tower!" He held the pistol to my head and nodded towards the tower on the hill top. "Off you go, lad."

I paused at the door to the barn and looked at the actor. "Thanks, Hugh. Thanks very much," I said bitterly.

CHAPTER SIXTEEN

"Enter, sir, the castle"

"Interesting house you have here," Hugh said as we walked behind Nebless Clem Croser. Our hands were tied in front of us and the rope was attached to the old Reiver's saddle.

"This is how Forster and Marsden used to take their prisoners back to England," the man said, ignoring Hugh's remark. "You're lucky you only have to walk half a Scottish mile. We had to walk twenty miles a day. If you stumbled, you were dragged along until you got back to your feet."

"That must have been painful!" Hugh exclaimed.

"Aye," the man said. "But they reckon it's more painful when the rope's around your neck." He turned around and leered at us. "No doubt you'll be able to tell us tomorrow, eh?"

"Why wait until tomorrow?" I asked.

He stopped the horse and turned again. "I'm not a murderer. I'll get the King's warrant to have you executed as spies. Your deaths will be perfectly legal."

"That's good to know," I said. I didn't say what had struck me most about his comment. I wanted to keep it secret for now. I should have guessed that Hugh would spill the secret like an overturned mug of ale.

"But the King's in Edinburgh!" he said. "You can't get to Edinburgh and back in a day!"

Nebless Clem clamped his mouth tight shut, and turned and kicked his horse into a steady amble so that we had to run to keep up with him. "Hugh!" I panted. "Can't you think before you speak, just for once."

"What have I said?"

"If King James is within half a day's ride of the Borders then he isn't in Edinburgh."

"Where is he?" said Hugh, surprised.

"He's close by!"

"John Forster doesn't know that, or he'd have told us," said Hugh, as we trotted along the dusty path and slowed as we reached a gate.

"Of course he doesn't. Don't you see? That's part of the secret. There's something going on in the Border region and you've been sent to find out what it is. You have another clue. It involves King James VI!"

Hugh looked at me with admiration. "I say, young Will! That's clever. You'd make a wonderful spy."

"Better than some," I thought bitterly.

"Welcome to Windy Gyle Pele Tower," the rider said. "Have you ever been to a Pele Tower before, Master Spy?"

"No, but I've been to the Tower of London," he said.

Nebless Clem climbed down, looked at his home proudly and said, "You won't find a safer fortress in the world than a Border Pele." Then he added, "Of course, the Scottish ones are better than the English ones."

"Of course," Hugh said politely.

"This wall is the height of three men and as thick as a man's stride. In these parts we call it a Barmkin wall. When you English robbers attack us, we bring the cattle inside here."

He led the way through the sturdy oak gate into a large

earth yard. Small buildings stood against the inside of the wall. They were houses for servants, cattle sheds and stables. In the middle of the yard stood the massive stone tower itself.

Nebless Clem passed his horse to a servant and took the ropes in his own hands to lead us through a small thick door into the tower. The room took up the whole of the ground floor. The damp walls were bare apart from metal rings for tying up animals. "If the English get over the wall, we bring the animals in here and lock that door. If they try to get in the door, they'll have to deal with whatever we throw at them from the top of the tower. Then there's a second iron door here," he said, opening a metal grating. "We call this the yett."

"But they could get in," Hugh said, "in the end."

"They could," the Scot agreed, leading us up a spiral stairway that climbed to the floor above. "But we live on the next floor, and we just block this stairway with boulders and benches and close the trapdoor."

"Ingenious," Hugh said.

The room that we climbed into was dark with narrow slit windows and a roaring fire in a huge open fireplace giving the only light. The furniture was heavy and plain. There were no tapestries on the walls or carpets on the floor as we had at Marsden Hall. "Very cosy," Hugh said.

Nebless Clem glared at him and, like my grandfather, suspected that he was being made fun of by the young man. "Aye. Sadly there's no fire in the room above. You may be a little cold tonight."

A second spiral stairway led to the top room. Sacks and chests showed that this was where food and weapons were stored. The Reiver nodded towards a small square room at the side. A wooden board with a hole in the middle rested over a gap in the stonework. "That's where you do your business," he said.

"Very useful to know," Hugh said.

"And this ladder leads up to the roof," Clem explained finally. "But I'll be taking the ladder away and the door to the roof is locked anyway." He looked around, satisfied. "The perfect castle for a poor Border farmer like myself when those English vermin try to rob me and my people in the village."

"It's a difficult place to get into," Hugh admitted.

"I think you'll find, Master Spy, that it is also a very difficult place to get out of."

"I wouldn't think of trying!" Hugh said.

"You wouldn't?"

"No! Once you've seen the King and explained that we are a couple of harmless actors I am sure he'll tell you to release us!"

For the first time since we'd arrived Clem looked uncertain. It was almost as if he believed the story. "I'll be back tomorrow morning," he said. "One of my men will be up later to take that ladder down and bring you a little supper. I'd never hang a man on an empty stomach."

"That's very thoughtful of you," I said sourly.

"Very thoughtful," Hugh agreed. I think he meant it.

I went to the narrow window and looked out on to the darkening moors around the village. The tower was in a perfect position to see riders approaching from miles away. A distant forest was almost ink-dark now, but I could make out a lighter shape moving against its dark background. It was a small pony ridden by someone small. I knew it was the boy in the cap. I knew that when he reported to Nebless Clem, our death warrants would be sealed. I sighed.

"What can you see?" Hugh asked.

"Ah! I – ah! I can see Clem and a couple of his men riding out of the Barmkin wall." I walked across to the next narrow window. "I think that's north. He's heading north."

"It'll be dark soon," the spy said.

"Yes. King James must be fairly close."

"I wish I could get to meet the King," Hugh said. "I was really looking forward to performing for him."

It was hard to believe what I was hearing. "Hugh," I said patiently, "you are not here to act for the King. You are here to spy on him."

"Ah, yes, of course," he said. "But I could give a performance of Mercutio's speech from Mr Shakespeare's *Romeo and Juliet* while I was spying, couldn't I?"

"No, Hugh," I said, heavily. "I think spies are supposed to be secret. Like the dentist that John Forster arrested."

"Bit late for secrecy now," he sighed.

I was watching the boy on the pony. He wasn't riding towards the village and he wasn't riding after Nebless Clem. He was staying in the shadow of the trees as if he were waiting for something. I couldn't imagine what it might be. Why didn't he just ride into the village and say what he knew from the time he'd picked up our trail back at Marsden? The thought of Marsden Manor, my family – even Meg – made me sad suddenly. I wanted to die of old age in my bed in Marsden Manor. I didn't want to die at the end of a rope, hanging from some dismal tower in this place that God had forgotten about.

Grandfather wanted to die a hero's death. Let him. He'd had his life. I'd seen nothing and done nothing.

"Shall I recite a speech from Mr Shakespeare's play Richard II?" Hugh asked. He walked to the centre of the room and began:

"For God's sake, let us sit upon the ground
And tell sad stories of the death of kings
How some have been deposed, some slain in war,
Some haunted by the ghosts they have deposed,
Some poisoned by their wives, some sleeping killed.
All murdered."

I wondered how Anne Boleyn and Katherine Howard had felt the night before their executions. I wondered if they had felt the sense of loss and waste that I was feeling. They must have done. And I wondered if they had cried.

I was swallowed up in self-pity and glad that the darkness hid the tears that scalded my cheeks.

Some time later a guard brought food and took away the ladder to the roof. I had climbed it earlier and saw that there was no way through the trapdoor on to the roof. Not without tools. I searched through the weapon chests and found some pikes that might have been useful. But without the ladder to reach the door it was hopeless.

I ate the thin broth that the guard brought and lay back on some of the grain sacks. Despite all my fears and worries I fell asleep quickly and deeply. It was some time far into the night that Hugh Richmond woke me by shaking my shoulder and hissing in my ear, "Will!"

"What?" I was cold and didn't want to be woken.

"Will, there's a noise coming from the roof."

"Rats," I said.

"No, rats don't have tools. It sounds like metal on stone."

I sat up, slowly coming awake and hearing the soft grate of iron against the stone slabs of the roof. The quarter moon gave very little light, but I thought I saw the edge of a knife slide under a slab and begin to lift it. The stone creaked as the nails were torn out of the roof beams. Then a hand reached into the gap in the trapdoor and pulled. I saw a patch of stars glitter through the gap now and the silhouette of the figure that owned the knife.

"Someone come to rescue us," Hugh said.

"More likely someone to murder us. Only the Scots know we're here," I said.

"Shh!" the voice hissed from the roof.

The slab was moved slowly and quietly from its place till a large square let in the faint moonlight. The figure disappeared for a few moments, then returned and dropped a rope down into the room. Then our visitor gripped the rope and swung himself down hand over hand. Even in the dim light I knew it was the boy who'd been following us for days.

Nebless Clem was so sure that we couldn't escape that he'd allowed us to keep our knives. I reached to my belt and gripped mine now. I slid it from the sheath and prepared to strike.

"What have you come for?" I asked. I pointed the blade upwards, ready to hit the stranger in the heart if he made a move to harm us. I couldn't see his face under the wide cap, but his eyes caught some of the starlight and reflected it back to me. They were looking straight into mine.

"I've come to rescue you, of course, you bufflehead!"

"Meg!" I said with a sob. "Is that you, Meg?"

"That's right. And it's just like you said. This is no place for a girl, so why don't we get out?"

She took her cap off and I could see her grin, ice-white in the moonlight. There were a thousand questions in my head, but not one word could get past the lump I felt in my throat. I simply put both arms around her and held her very, very tightly. I was terrified that this was a dream and that she'd be gone if I let go and woke up.

CHAPTER SEVENTEEN

"The night is long that never finds the day"

"Where did you learn to climb like that?" I asked Meg when I finally let her go.

"Climbing the cliffs at the coast looking for seagull eggs," she explained. "After Roker Cliffs, climbing a Pele Tower is as easy as a flight of stairs."

"You left it late," Hugh complained, a little ungratefully.

"I had to ride round the village in a large circle, then wait till it got dark," she said. "I suppose you'd have walked through the village in broad daylight?"

"He did," I muttered.

Meg told us to arm ourselves with some of the weapons from the storeroom and take some of the Scottish steel bonnets and cloaks with us. "If we're riding through Scotland, it'll be better if we look Scots even from a distance."

"We don't sound Scots though," I said gloomily. "It was our speech that trapped us in this village. As soon as we open our mouths, we'll give ourselves away."

Then a voice came through the darkness that I'll swear made my heart stop beating for several seconds. "You'll hang from my tower this very night and your eyes will be food for the crows," the voice said, in its strong Scots accent.

I gripped Meg's wrist. "Nebless Clem!" I whispered. "I'd know his voice anywhere."

Then Hugh Richmond said, "Actually it was me."

I breathed again and Meg shook her wrist free from my grasp. "That's amazing!" I said.

"I'm an actor," he said. "It's my job to listen to people and copy their voices and their movements. Clem's easy!"

"Then there's a chance for us," Meg breathed.

"How?" I asked.

"Let's get out of here first, then I'll explain."

We made two journeys up and down the rope, passing lances and steel bonnets and clothing up to the roof. Then we lowered the rope over the edge of the tower. Meg climbed down, we tied the weapons and clothes into bundles and lowered them down to her. Finally Hugh and I slid down.

We hurried through the yard to the gate in the Barmkin wall. The bolts were well greased and slid open easily. "No guards?" I wondered.

"Who wants to stay out here in the cold and dark?" Meg asked. "They stay in the tower and look out for beacon fires from time to time."

We padded down the silent road past the miserable little houses to where our horses were grazing in the field behind the barn. The saddles and packs were in the barn where we'd left them. As I opened the barn door there was a rushing and scuttering of feet followed by a furious barking. The rat-catchers were on duty.

Somewhere nearby a shutter opened and a voice called, "Who's there?"

"It's only me, Clem Croser," Hugh called back.

"Sorry, sir," the voice called and we heard the shutter close. Meg calmed the dog while Hugh and I groped in the corner for our saddles. Ten minutes later we were riding out of the village along the road that Nebless Clem had taken.

There was enough moonlight to see the track, but we didn't dare go too fast. We climbed out of the valley and reached the crest of a hill. Behind us to the south there were beacons burning in a string like amber beads. "Large raid in England again," I said. "Why are there so many raids all of a sudden?"

"Perhaps we'll find out tomorrow," Meg said.

As we wound our way down into the next valley she described how she'd followed us all the way from Marsden Manor and how she'd laughed at our attempts to shake her off. "Wat Grey back at Marsden village showed me how to follow hoof prints for when his horses strayed. Even when you were out of sight I could follow your trail," she explained.

"Just as well for us," Hugh said.

"So what's your plan, Master Richmond?" she asked.

"He hasn't got one," I told her.

"Ah, young Will, but I have the seed of an idea growing in my brain!"

"Then let's hope the Scots don't chop it from your shoulders before the seed grows," I said irritably.

Hugh was about to explain his plan when Meg hissed, "Listen!"

We stopped our ponies on the edge of a gaunt clump of trees. The ground was trembling and there was a faint rumbling sound. As it grew louder we could hear the cry of complaining cattle. "It's a reive," Meg said. "It's coming this way."

"Then all we have to do is follow them. See where they're headed."

"The last group of troopers to follow a raid never returned," Meg reminded me.

"Ah, but they didn't have the Queen's spy with the germ of a plan in his head," I told her.

"That's true," Hugh said. "Let's hide in those trees till they go past."

The ponies plodded into the shadow of the trees just before the first rider came past. I looked for the steel bonnet in the moonlight, but didn't see it. His head was bare and his long hair and beard streamed like a banner in the west wind. The man was different from Nebless Clem's Border Reivers. Instead of a jack he was wearing a light tunic. I thought it might have been yellow or light brown. And strapped across his back was the largest sword I've ever seen.

About a hundred cattle trotted behind him and were driven from behind by more of the strange men with the yellow tunics and the mighty swords.

When the last one had passed we moved carefully out of the cover of the trees. Hugh began to kick his pony into a faster walk, but Meg said, "There's no need to hurry. I can follow a trail like that with my eyes closed."

"Who were those men?" Hugh asked.

"Reivers," Meg said.

"No," I said. "My grandfather described men like that to me when he told us about Flodden."

"That's right!" Meg cried. "They're Highlanders! Those big swords are what they call claymores."

"If the Highlanders have come down to the Borders, that explains why there's been so much thieving. They need to keep themselves supplied with food," I said. "That solves part of the mystery. They're also kidnapping anyone who tries to follow them. That explains the other part of the mystery."

"No, it doesn't," Hugh said. "I mean, why on earth are they here? The Highlanders and the borderers don't even like one another. And why do they need to keep it such a secret?"

"That's your job to find out," Meg said.

"True," the young man sighed and we rode on in silence.

When the sun began to rise it was blood red, glowing through a light autumn mist. The trail of the stolen cattle was clear on the ground. We came over a rise and looked down into a valley. A rough wood and turf hut had been put up at the entrance to the valley. About ten borderers with their steel bonnets stood around a fire and were roasting strips of meat on the ends of their daggers.

"We must be close. They have the road guarded," I said.

"We could go around them," Meg said.

"They must have thought of that," I sighed. "Whatever they're hiding will be guarded on all sides. Those are Border men down there. They'll know every path into that valley like I know the garden at Marsden Hall."

Hugh rubbed his hands together briskly. "Then it's just as well I have a plan."

"Kill the guards?" Meg said.

"Certainly not!" Hugh said. "You are a terribly violent child."

"Maybe we should ride down and let them kill us instead," Meg snapped.

"Yes, we'll ride down," Hugh said. Suddenly he switched to his Nebless Clem voice. "But they won't kill one of their own Scots Reiver friends, will they?"

"Fine," Meg said. "But William and I can't talk like that."

"No," Hugh said. "You are English. I've just captured

you and I'm taking you in to be questioned by the King himself."

"But if the King's there he'll hang us!" I objected.

Hugh spread his hands wide. "That's a chance we'll have to take!"

"No!" I told him angrily. "It's a chance Meg and I will have to take!"

"Have you got a better plan?" he asked.

The Reivers at the guard post had noticed us now and were gathering their weapons. Meg took the rope from her saddle, wound it quickly round my wrists then ordered Hugh to tie her hands too. As the Reivers lined up to face us Hugh led us down towards them.

"What have you got there, friend?" the sergeant of the Reivers cried when we were twenty paces away.

"Two wee English lads that strayed over the border," Hugh said in his Scots accent. "I think they may be spies."

"Aye," the sergeant said and spat on the ground. "That's just like the English. Using bairns to do a man's work."

"Well, these two won't grow to be men!" Hugh said with a harsh laugh. "By tonight they'll be swinging from a tree and the crows will have their eyes!"

The guards laughed. I muttered, "I wish he wouldn't keep saying that!"

Hugh tugged on the rope and led us forward. The line of Reivers parted to let us through. When we were into the valley the sergeant called after us, "By the way!"

Hugh turned. "Aye?"

"What's the password? I forgot to ask you."

"I only know yesterday's password because I've been out of the camp. You'll have to tell me today's password."

"It's 'Remember Bannockburn'!" the sergeant shouted helpfully.

"Aye! Remember Bannockburn!" said Hugh. "A terrible defeat."

"We won!" the sergeant said.

"Aye – you did – we did," Hugh laughed. "I meant a terrible defeat for the English rabble."

The sergeant just nodded and turned back to the meat that he'd left roasting by the edge of the fire. It smelled good, but I had no appetite. We rode on, then came to a smaller valley that led off this one. This was guarded too, and now we could see why. Hundreds of tents of all sizes covered the floor of the valley and stretched halfway up the slopes.

There must have been thousands of men there. Highlanders in their yellow shirts and Reivers in their jacks, as well as knights with their richly coloured tunics showing a zoo of lions and eagles and dragons.

Most of the tents were a dull grey, but some were made of richer silks and had banners fluttering in the light September morning breeze. Even at this early hour men were practising their drill and training with weapons. The Highlanders seemed to keep themselves apart, fighting furiously with their claymores while the Border men packed into tight rows with pikes bristling and reflecting back the blood-red rays of the sun.

Squires were hurrying after knights, carrying armour, leading war horses and carrying food into the silk tents. The guards at this entrance were more alert than at the outpost. "Password?" their sergeant demanded.

"Remember Bannockburn," Hugh said.

"Who are the prisoners?"

"English spies. I was told to take them to the King."

The sergeant had thick black brows that almost vanished into the peak of his steel bonnet when he heard this.

"The King wants to see two boys?"

"That's what I was told," Hugh said.

"Then why are they wearing daggers?" the man scowled. "You must know King James has a terror of being assassinated. That's why he wears that padded jacket."

"Of course," Hugh said, as he slid the weapons from our belts. "I'll mention your sharp eyes to the King."

The man's scowl disappeared. "I'll take you to his tent myself," he offered. "I hope he's awake. He was drinking late into the night with his officers."

We dismounted and handed the ponies to one of the soldiers. With the ropes around our wrists Hugh led us into the valley after the sergeant and through the crowds of men, who scarcely noticed us. The King's tent was the largest and the cloth of gold banner above it had the blood-red lion of Scotland painted on it. The lion rippled like a living beast. I wondered if its owner would have us torn apart.

Hugh's idea suddenly seemed mad. What on earth was he hoping to gain from this? And how were we going to escape with our lives? He'd already led us into Nebless Clem Croser's prison. Now he was leading us into the lion's den itself.

There were two well-armed knights at the entrance to the King's tent. They stopped the sergeant and asked what his business was.

"This man's brought two English spies in for the King to question."

"We haven't heard about this."

"Nebless Clem Croser of Windy Gyle captured them," Hugh explained.

"That's right. He came in last night to report it," said

one of the knights to the other. He looked at us carefully. "But I thought he said it was a simple-minded English spy and a boy."

"Ah!" Hugh smiled, and for a moment I saw the blankness at the back of his eyes. The blankness of the actor who's forgotten his lines.

I stepped forward. "I am not simple-minded," I said. "And this boy as you call him," I added, nodding towards Meg, "is none other than the son of Sir James Marsden of Marsden Manor in Durham."

"But Clem Croser said it was a man," the knight insisted.

"He said that because he wanted to make the King think he'd captured someone more dangerous."

The knight gave a snort. "That sounds like the old rogue. I'll ask if the King wants to question you before we hang you," he said and turned away. That word "hang" made my throat go tight and my stomach feel sick every time I heard it.

Hugh winked at me happily. "Quick thinking there, young Will. We'll make an actor of you yet!"

"If I live long enough," I grumbled.

The knight came out of the tent and said, "The King is dressing. He'll see you in a moment. Step into the entrance to the tent." Hugh took a step forward and the knight moved across to block his path. "Not you."

"But I captured the young villains."

"I thought Clem Croser captured them."

"Ah – he – I delivered them to him for safekeeping. But I was the one who first laid hands on them."

"You will be rewarded, no doubt. But the King doesn't need you in there now."

"But – "

"His Majesty is very nervous about strange men who come near him fully armed."

"I'm a loyal subject!" Hugh objected.

"That's what the priest said who came to pray for James III – and look what happened with him!"

"What?" Hugh asked.

I shut my eyes. Hugh just couldn't help saying a word or two too many.

"Don't you know your Scottish history, man?" the knight asked quietly and stepped forward for a closer look at the spy.

Hugh gave a foolish grin. "Yes!" he lied.

I dug deep into my memory and tried to remember one of Grandfather's stories. "Even in England we know about James III," I said.

"Do we?" Hugh asked, surprised.

"We know that he was wounded in a battle with his son," I said quickly. "A priest came to the King's sick bed. But when he knelt to pray he pulled out a knife and stabbed the King to death."

The knight glared at Hugh. "You should be ashamed of yourself. Taking history lessons from a boy."

"Deeply, terribly ashamed," Hugh said weakly. He could clearly think of no reason to join us in the tent.

The knight pushed Meg and me forward. Hugh simply said, "The best of luck!" He was even losing his Scots accent.

A squire stepped from the inner tent and said, "The King will see the prisoners now."

CHAPTER EIGHTEEN

"Hang out our banners on the outward walls"

I thought I knew what to expect. I had heard my grand-parents' stories of Henry VIII and my mother's tales of Elizabeth I. I had seen the blood-red lion on the golden banner and the fine warriors who guarded him. The King of Scotland himself must be magnificent.

The inside of the tent glowed with a curious orange light as the morning sun filtered through the yellow silk walls. I could see a man sitting on a wooden stool and guessed he must be the King's secretary. He had an ugly face with watery eyes that bulged too much. He picked up a wine goblet and supped from it, dribbling wine from the side of his mouth. He wiped it away with a hand that was covered in a dark glove. He used the back of the same hand to wipe his nose. He sniffed loudly.

When he spoke, his voice was high and piping; the Scots accent was stronger than Nebless Clem's. "What?" I said.

He spoke a little more slowly, leaning forward and spraying my face with wine flecks from his blubbery lips. "I said, 'Do you not kneel before a king, you English?'"

"Where is he?" I asked.

The man jabbed a finger at his heavily padded black doublet. "I am the King! Kneel, you miserable English boy."

I dropped to one knee in shock as much as anything. I saw Meg begin to curtsey, remember who she was supposed to be and drop beside me. "I am sorry, Your Majesty," I said.

"Aye, well, it's dim in here. It's an easy mistake to make," he said, and chuckled. "Stand up now while I question you. Now, they tell me you are English spies, is that right?"

I was about to answer when Meg said, "No. We were travelling up from Alnwick to Berwick when we took a wrong road and crossed the border by mistake."

"I see!" King James said. "You hope to save your necks with lies like that, do you?"

"Yes. I mean it's not a lie," I said.

"Two young people. Travelling alone? Why would you be doing that?"

It was a good question. I hadn't thought of the answer, but as I began to speak the story came out. I guessed this was what Hugh Richmond meant by "making it up as you go along". I hardly believed it was my own voice speaking the words. "We were travelling ahead to arrange lodgings for my grandfather in Berwick," I said. "He's very old and we didn't want to arrive there with no place for him to stay."

"And your grandfather's name?"

"Sir Clifford Marsden," I said.

"Ah, from the Marsden Estates in Durham, would that be?" he asked.

"You know about Marsden Manor?" I said. My surprise was not an act this time.

The King looked pleased with himself. He sipped his wine again and wiped his wet mouth noisily. "I know a lot about England. I have my own spies, you know. I want to know who supports me when I take old Queen Bess's throne. And I want to know who will try to oppose me. They tell me the Marsden family has always supported the Tudors, is that right?"

"Yes, Your Majesty."

"And a Marsden has fought in every battle against my country for the last hundred years."

"Yes, Your Majesty."

"So you must be trembling at the thought of me being your new King when the old Queen passes away?"

"Yes, Your Majesty."

"So you will do anything to stop me taking the English throne. You will even send old men and children to spy on me."

"Old men?" I said.

"That's right. Sir Clifford Marsden. Your grandfather. My agent in Durham says he set off with one of Queen Elizabeth's spies and with his grandson last week." James looked carefully at Meg. "My spy said nothing about this boy, though."

I felt my chances of staying alive were slipping away. At least I might be able to save Meg. "He's not a boy, Your Majesty. He's a serving girl. Her name is Meg and she isn't part of any plot to spy on you."

"Very noble of you to say so," James said. "But you see why I can't set her free, don't you?"

"No?" I said.

Meg stepped forward. "Because I know his secret," she said simply.

"What is my secret?" James asked.

"Queen Elizabeth won't announce that you are to be king when she dies. She thinks everyone will turn away from her and crown you before she's even dead. So you've decided that if she won't hand you the throne, you'll just take it."

James gave a crooked smile. "And what makes you think that?" he asked.

"The Highlanders," Meg said. "They are your fiercest fighters. They're the ones that terrify the English most. You wouldn't bring them all the way from the Highlands if you didn't plan to invade."

"You're a clever young lady. Cleverer than that spy of Queen Elizabeth's. But perhaps I am simply training my army here on the Borders. Perhaps I am sending my soldiers abroad to help our friends in France? Eh? You never thought of that, did you?" he cackled, jabbing the dirty glove at her.

"If you were training your army you wouldn't be so secretive about it," said Meg. "The Highlanders came down here and started raiding over the English border for food. As soon as the wardens sent a hot trod after them, you knew they'd see the army you gathered here. That's why you massacred them."

James frowned. "You're right and you're wrong, young Meg. Yes, the Highlanders have been raiding your farms. But I haven't massacred the Moss Troopers that followed them back! I just sent them up to Edinburgh Castle under guard. You have to remember, I'm going to be your king soon. I don't want your people to see me as a murderer. I'm not like your Henry VIII!"

The King stood up and began to pace across the carpet that had been laid in the tent. His voice was higher than ever and angry. "Your Henry killed my great-grandfather at Flodden Field and he killed my grandfather at Solway Moss. Your Queen Elizabeth had my mother's head cut off. But I am not a vengeful man. I am not like you

English, though God knows I have reason enough to be."

"So you'll set us free?" Meg asked quietly.

The King stopped pacing and looked at her sadly. He lowered his eyes, unable to stand her gaze. "No, I can't do that."

"So we have to die," I said.

Before he could answer the knight who guarded the door entered and bowed. "Sorry, Your Majesty, but we have arrested the other two spies. The two old men on the road from Alnwick to Berwick."

"Sir Clifford Marsden and Sir John Forster?" James asked.

"Yes, Your Majesty."

"Bring them here," he ordered and rubbed his gloves together in satisfaction. "All the snakes from the nest in the same bag," he said.

CHAPTER NINETEEN

"I'll fight till from my bones my flesh be hacked"

It broke my heart to see my grandfather dragged into the tent. The sun was stronger and the light was bright yellow now, but it couldn't hide the greyness of the old man's face. He sank on to a stool and looked up at me. He made a faint effort at a smile. "Sorry, William," he said.

I knew it was Hugh Richmond's fault that all King James's "snakes" had ended up here. I just shook my head.

Meg said, "Can Sir Clifford have a drink of wine?" Almost before the King had agreed she took the flask from the table and handed it to my grandfather. He took a deep drink, then seemed to recover some spirit. Sir John Forster, looking almost as weary, was brought to stand at the door.

"Now, my friends, we can have the truth at last!" the King said gleefully.

"We were all heading to Berwick when we got lost," I said.

Sir John said angrily, "Sir Clifford and I didn't get lost. We were clearly on the road to Berwick when a gang of Scottish rogues snatched us and dragged us across the border. This is kidnap and it is illegal!"

The King waved a limp hand. "You gentlemen were brought here to be witnesses in the trial of these young spies. If your answers displease me, I will hang them and let you go. And there is nothing illegal about that. Do you understand?"

"Aye," said Grandfather.

"So," the King said, "you were not on a trip to Berwick, you were trying to find out what my plans were."

"That's right," Grandfather said. "Over two hundred Englishmen have disappeared. We were sent to find out where they had gone. Our queen has a right to know."

"They crossed the border and were imprisoned, you can tell her."

Sir John Forster cut in angrily, "There has always been an agreement that Moss Troopers can cross the border in pursuit of cattle Reivers. They weren't attacking Scotland, they were simply following a hot trod."

James shrugged his heavy, padded shoulders. "Sadly they followed the thieves to this camp and saw our preparations. I could not let them return."

"You can if you give up this foolish idea of an invasion," said Grandfather.

The Scottish King sat opposite him and rested his bearded chin on a fist. "Now, you're an old and respected soldier, Sir Clifford. I would like to know why you think an invasion would be 'foolish'."

Grandfather looked at him uncertainly, but the King seemed as if he really wanted the old man's opinion. "James IV failed at Flodden," he said.

James rubbed his hands as if he were enjoying himself. "You know your history, Sir Clifford, but so do I. James IV failed because he came down off Branxton Ridge. If he'd stayed there he'd have won."

"You Scots have problems with your Highland troops. Brave fighters but they don't like straying too far from home. When you go into England, they will raid and burn and loot and kill. Then they'll head home with their prizes and desert you. They did that to your great-grandfather and they'll do it to you."

"I know," the King said softly. "But I still have my borderers."

"And what did they do at Flodden? They started looting the corpses on the battlefield – English and Scottish dead – when they should have been carrying on with the fight. They are robbers by nature, not soldiers."

"I know. But I have five hundred of the best knights ever to set foot on a battlefield."

"But they may be faced by twice as many English knights."

The smile slid from the King's lips. "The English have not got time to gather their knights together. That's why it's so important for this invasion to remain a secret till it happens."

Grandfather rose slowly and painfully to his feet. Meg reached out a hand to steady him. "Your Majesty," Grandfather said, "I myself have seen over one thousand English knights, fully armed and gathered in one great field."

"Where?" King James asked suspiciously.

"At York."

The king's face fell and his lips began to work nervously. He walked across to the door and called, "Croser!"

A moment later the old Scottish Reiver walked in. He looked at Grandfather and Sir John with loathing, then stood next to his king. "Croser," the King said, "you know this man?"

"Aye. Know him and love him like I love toad-poison."

"But is he a man of his word?"

"He is an Englishman and so he must be a liar," Croser spat.

"If I had a sword I'd kill you for that remark," Sir John said.

"You'd be welcome to try," Croser sneered.

"Gentlemen! You are not squabbling boys!" the King cut in. "This is a matter too serious for your little jealousies and hatreds. Now, Croser, Sir Clifford says he has seen a thousand English knights gathered at York. Can I believe him?"

"The old English lie," Nebless Clem breathed. "Solway Moss, all those years ago. Remember, Sir John?"

"I remember."

"We asked if you had more men behind you. What did you say?"

"I said there were ten thousand men behind us."

"And how many were there?"

"None."

The old Reiver nodded. He had waited sixty years to avenge himself for that lie. "Never believe an Englishman."

Grandfather said, "But if I had a Bible I could swear on anything you like that what I said is true."

James looked at him. He walked across to a metal-studded oak chest in the corner of his tent. He pulled out a book covered in black leather. "Here's my Bible, Sir Clifford." He placed it on the table. "Your knife, Croser," he ordered.

The Reiver passed his blade across to his king. James lunged forward and took me by the arm in a grip like an eagle's claw. He thrust the knife against my throat. I felt its sharp coldness and the pain of the tip pricking at my skin. "Swear on the life of your grandson, Sir Clifford. I am a king. I represent God on this earth. If you lie on God's Bible then He will guide this hand of mine to spill the boy's blood."

"I know," my grandfather said.

"And are you still ready to swear the oath?" the King asked. In his excitement the hand that held the knife was trembling.

"I am."

Grandfather was going to lie. God was going to punish *him* by killing *me*. I closed my eyes and muttered a jumble of prayers. "Don't lie, Grandfather," I gasped.

"I won't," he said. "I would gladly risk my own life for my country. I would never risk yours."

He stepped towards the table and placed his right hand on the black book. "I solemnly swear that I told the truth … I told the truth when I said that I have seen a thousand fully-armed English knights at York."

There was no sound inside the tent. Only the muffled noises of men and horses from outside. The knife trembled. It pressed more firmly against my skin. Then, slowly – painfully slowly – the knife moved away.

"You see, Croser, Sir Clifford is telling the truth."

"Aye. He is," the old cattle-thief agreed.

The King calmly handed back the knife and sat on his stool. I was wishing that I too had something to collapse on to. My knees were weak and my heart thumping.

"What you have guessed about the invasion," said King James, "It is all true. Some of my lords in Edinburgh are impatient. They can't wait for old Queen Bess to die. So I put on this show to keep them happy, you understand."

"I understand," Grandfather said.

"They want to win themselves glory by fighting against the old enemy. And some of the older ones, like Croser here, simply want revenge."

"I know," Grandfather agreed. "But if you wait, the throne will become yours. If you invade – and if you lose – the English will close the border to you forever. I have heard you like horse-racing, Your Majesty?"

James grinned. "Aye, I do."

"A war against England is a two-horse race and you could lose your money. You tried to give the Scottish horse a half-mile start by this surprise. But the longer the race goes on, then the greater your chances of losing."

"I have thought of that, Sir Clifford."

"Why not bet on the race with just one horse? The one that you will ride into England when Queen Elizabeth dies? No one lives forever."

"You're a wise man, Sir Clifford."

"No. I'm just a very old man."

"So is my friend Croser here," the King said, turning to the Reiver. "What do you think, Clem?"

"I hope I live long enough to ride behind you when you ride into England," he said and his smile was grim.

"You want your revenge? You want to destroy Marsden Manor and leave it like a smoking desert, don't you?"

The man bowed his head. "I did want that, yes. But I've seen so much blood spilt in the name of revenge. So many houses burned to the ground. So many widows and so many orphans. I'll always hate you, Sir Clifford – I'll always hate all the English, and you especially, Sir John. But there's no glory in killing old men and children."

Grandfather took a step towards him. "I hate you too, Clem Croser," he said with a strange smile. He stretched out his right hand. Slowly the Reiver raised a hand. First he grasped my grandfather's hand with his right hand and then with both hands. Finally he pulled the old man towards him and wrapped both arms around him.

The Reiver looked up, loosened one arm and held it out towards Sir John Forster. The old enemy crossed the floor and joined in the embrace.

King James looked at Meg and me. "Maybe there is hope for my idea of a United Kingdom after all. Maybe the red lion of Scotland can wear the gold crown of England and bring peace."

"The red and the gold," Meg said. "They go well together."

CHAPTER TWENTY

"Light thickens, and the crow makes wing towards the rocky wood"

The journey back to Marsden Manor was slow and, for Grandfather at least, painful. We made barely ten miles a day. But he didn't seem to mind the pain. He was at peace with himself.

"You wanted to do one last great deed before you died, Grandfather," I said as we rode side by side from Alnwick after saying goodbye to Sir John Forster.

"I did want that," he agreed.

"You've saved Marsden Manor from avenging Scots when King James takes the crown."

"I saved it for you, my boy."

"And saving your nation from a bloody war is the greatest deed ever," I told him.

"Even if he did have to do it with a lie!" Meg laughed.

I stopped my pony and looked at her. "There was no lie!" I said.

"There aren't a thousand English knights at York!" she cried.

"You weren't with us when we first arrived at Alnwick Castle on the journey up to Scotland," I reminded her.

"So?"

"So Grandfather told us the story of his meeting with Henry VIII and Katherine Howard at York. Old Henry wanted to show his force to James V. So he took a thousand knights with him and they camped in the fields outside the city walls."

"That was years ago!" Meg objected.

"I know."

"But King James thought your grandfather meant now!"

"Did he really? Maybe James isn't as close to God as he likes to believe. As I remember, Grandfather said, 'I have seen a thousand English knights at York.' And it was perfectly true. He just forgot to say when he'd seen them."

Meg screwed up her small face into a frown. "That's cheating!"

"Clem Croser always said that about me shooting him in the back," Grandfather laughed. "But if you do something for the right reason then I'm sure a little cheating does no harm."

"Did you know Sir Clifford was telling the truth when the King had the knife at your throat?" Meg asked me.

"Of course."

"So why did you look so scared?" she jeered.

"I was acting," I said.

"Then you're the best actor I've ever seen."

Hugh Richmond had been quiet for most of the journey. "Yes, young Will is a good actor."

"Will you introduce me to a company in London?" I whispered so that Grandfather couldn't hear as he rode ahead.

"Certainly. It's the least I can do. I owe you a lot, Will."

"Your acting was good," I grinned.

"But my spying was awful."

"True," Meg said, a little unkindly. But I remembered

that her life had been at risk because of Hugh's clumsiness.

"Stick to acting in future," I suggested.

"I think I will," he said. He cheered up a lot after that. He kept us entertained on the journey with stories and speeches from the plays of his Mr Shakespeare. At the taverns where we stopped each night he put on a performance for the locals and earned himself a purse full of silver.

When we finally reached the fork in the road that leads to Marsden Hall he left us to ride on to Lambton and report to his lordship. He shook hands with Grandfather and kissed Meg goodbye. Finally he turned to me. We shook hands and he held mine firmly, looking at me seriously. "You must come to London, Will," he said as the other two rode off out of earshot.

"One day," I said.

"Look for me in Mr Shakespeare's company. I will make sure he finds you a part in one of his plays."

"Thank you, Hugh, I will."

"But soon, Will. Make it soon. You're wasting your talent staying here on this manor."

"It's my home," I said.

"And it will still be here when you want to come back. Come to London."

"I will."

"Soon."

"Soon. I promise."

The actor grinned, gave a dramatic wave of his hand and bowed from the saddle before riding off.

I caught up with Meg and Grandfather and we rode slowly down the path that led to our home. Two women stood at the gateway to Marsden Hall. Grandmother, stiff and unsmiling, and Mother, quiet and content.

Grooms took the ponies from us and we walked into the

walled garden as the sun was setting.

Sometimes you get those perfect October days when the sky is so clear you can see halfway to heaven. Only the bare rose bushes showed that it would soon be winter. One last rose hung alone. "A red Tudor rose," Grandfather said. "Like Elizabeth, the last of the line. The end of a century, the end of a family, and the end of a great queen soon."

"But our family will go on, thanks to you," I said.

He looked pleased with that. Somewhere overhead a black bird croaked and began to circle the house. We all stopped and looked up. Grandmother began counting its circles.

"One," she said. "Three and it means a death."

"You said that last time," my mother said.

"Two," Grandmother said.

"Silly superstitious nonsense," my father grumbled, but he kept his eye on the bird as carefully as any of us.

"Three!"

The bird settled on the West Tower and looked down at us. "Who are you looking at, Mr Crow?" Grandmother cried. "Who will it be?"

"Awk!" the bird cried.

At that moment the kitchen door opened and Meg came out with a jug of wine and some goblets. "What are you looking at?" she asked.

"That unlucky crow up there. It circled three times around the house. Grandmother says that means a death," I explained.

Meg grinned widely. Her short hair made her look more like an elf than ever. "It always means that," she nodded. "Widow Atkinson says so, and she is never wrong."

"Never," I agreed.

"But do you see the bird's pale-blue eyes?" Meg asked.

"Yes."

"And the silver-grey neck?"

"Yes."

"That means it's a jackdaw and not a crow." She looked around at the worried faces of the family. "So that's all right, isn't it?"

"Oh!" I said.

"Awk!" the bird replied.

The Historical Characters

The Marsden family are fictional, but the main events of the story are true and so are several of the characters:

KING HENRY VIII 1491 – 1547 A ruthless king who always had to get his own way, no matter what the cost in human lives. The Catholic Church failed to give him a divorce from his first wife, so he created a new church and made himself head of it. He destroyed the monasteries and robbed them of their wealth; he made peace with the people who rebelled against this act ... then had them hanged.

CATHERINE OF ARAGON 1485 – 1536 A Spanish princess who was married to the son of the first Tudor king, Henry VII. Arthur died before he came to the throne, so she married his brother, Henry VIII. She was very popular with the English people, but Henry became bored with her and said they had never been really married, and that no man can marry his dead brother's bride. Catherine never gave up her claim to be queen. Henry hated her for that, imprisoned her and left her to die miserably.

ANNE BOLEYN c.1501 – 1536 An ambitious woman who made herself powerful by becoming Henry's second queen. Anne Boleyn hated his first queen and a lot of gossips blamed Anne for Catherine's death. Anne was the mother of Elizabeth, who became the last Tudor queen, but she failed to give Henry a son. He had her executed.

KATHERINE HOWARD died 1542 Lively young cousin of Anne Boleyn, who made the terrible mistake of marrying Henry when he was ageing and ill. When he discovered that she had been engaged before she met him, he was furious and had her executed.

SIR JOHN FORSTER 1501 – 1602 Sir John was the Warden of the English Border lands with Scotland, and knew the region better than anyone. He survived by being more cunning, treacherous and villainous than the criminals he was fighting against. Even at the end of his long life, gangs of criminals were plotting to kill him.

NEBLESS CLEM CROSER A Scottish cattle rustler who was raiding farms in the 1580s. "Nebless" means "nose-less" and we might guess that he lost his nose in one of the many fights cattle thieves got themselves into. We don't know much about Clem, but his history has been imagined in this story.

KING JAMES VI OF SCOTLAND 1566 – 1625 A strange man, whose mother was Mary, Queen of Scots. He became king at thirteen months old after Mary abdicated. He struggled to control his troublesome lords who wanted to run Scotland. His great ambition was to rule England when the last Tudor, Elizabeth died. In 1603 he took the throne of England and became James I of England. This brought peace between the countries, but neither country let him have his dream of a "United Kingdom" under one government.

The Time Trail

1485 Henry Tudor wins the English throne by defeating King Richard III in battle. He is crowned Henry VII and reigns until …

1509 Henry VII dies and his son becomes King Henry VIII. But …

1513 … Henry VIII wants to win glory by fighting the French. And, when Henry leaves England, the Scots attack in the north. They are defeated at Flodden Field and their king James IV dies. Seventeen-month-old James V takes the Scottish throne.

1520s The Borders become a lawless region with cattle thieves (called Reivers) raiding from both England and Scotland – but mostly from England. Back in England …

1536 … Henry's first wife, Catherine of Aragon, dies and his second, Anne Boleyn, is executed.

1537 Henry's third wife, Jane Seymour, dies soon after giving birth to his son, Edward.

1540 He marries Anna of Cleves, decides he hates her and divorces her so he can marry his fifth wife, Katherine Howard. Meanwhile ...

1541 ... Henry invites James V of Scotland to meet him in York to discuss peace. James fails to turn up and Henry is furious. He wants to destroy Scotland. But not before ...

1542 ... Henry has Katherine Howard executed. The English defeat James V at Solway Moss and the Scottish King dies. This is followed by ...

1543 ... the English attempt to destroy southern Scotland, until ...

1547 ... Henry VIII dies. Eventually ...

1558 ... Henry's daughter, the last Tudor, Elizabeth, comes to the throne and ...

1567 ... James VI becomes King of Scotland. As he grows up, he is friendly with Elizabeth even though ...

1587 ... Elizabeth executes James's mother, Mary Queen of Scots. Crafty James stays friendly because he knows that when ...

1603 ... Elizabeth dies, James becomes King of England. At last peace begins to come to the Borders.